Light from the oncoming car pierced the night, spreading in an ever-widening swath across the pavement behind her as it approached. She had to hide. But where?

The deeper darkness of a recessed doorway appeared on her left. She darted up the short flight of stairs, then wedged against the side wall as a long black car pulled up to the intersection. She grabbed the doorknob and gave it a violent twist. The latch clicked back as the gleam of the headlights threw her shadow against the painted wood. At that moment, she yanked the door open and leaped inside the building. She slammed the door closed and collapsed against it, her chest heaving with silent sobs.

"Good evening."

She jerked upright as an elderly man smiled and handed her a leaflet. In the center of the cover was a large cross with the word *Crossroads* emblazoned on the horizontal bar.

Hysterical laughter bubbled up in her throat. She was in a church. Of all places!

DOROTHY CLARK

is a creative person. She lives in a home she designed and helped her husband build (she swings a mean hammer!) with the able assistance of their three children. She also designs and helps her husband build furniture, and does remodeling and decorating for family and friends. When she is not thus engaged, she can be found cheering her grandchildren on at various sports events or band and chorus concerts, or furiously taking notes about possible settings for future novels as she and her husband travel throughout the United States and Canada. *Hosea's Bride* is Dorothy's debut novel. Her first historical romance, *Beauty for Ashes,* will be a June 2004 release from Steeple Hill Women's Fiction. Dorothy enjoys hearing from her readers, and may be contacted at dorothyjclark@hotmail.com.

HOSEA'S BRIDE

DOROTHY CLARK

Love Inspired.

Published by Steeple Hill Books™

STEEPLE HILL BOOKS

Steeple Hill®

ISBN 0-373-87260-7

HOSEA'S BRIDE

Copyright © 2004 by Dorothy Clark

Visit us at www.steeplehill.com

Printed in U.S.A.

And I will betroth thee unto Me for ever; yea, I will betroth thee unto Me in righteousness, and in judgment, and in lovingkindness, and in mercies. I will even betroth thee unto Me in faithfulness: and thou shalt know the LORD.

—*Hosea* 2:19-20

This book is lovingly dedicated to my best friend, hero and husband, Ralph; my children, Craig and Tina, Brenda and Jay, and Cory; my grandchildren, Megan, Shaina, Mason and Hillary. How could I ever write books about love without you in my life? You are all wonderful and special, and I love you to pieces. To my sisters Virginia and JoAnn, thanks for the prayers and support. Marjorie, thanks for those things *and* for being so careful of my time (Mt.10:41). To my nieces and nephews, thanks for rallying around, guys! I love you all. To Johnny, Orv, and Jody Kay, who live forever in my heart. And most of all to my Lord and Savior, Jesus Christ. Truly, in Him, all things are possible.

Special thanks to Pastor Ron Jutze and his wife, Shirley, for their unfailing love, support, encouragement and prayers on behalf of my writing ministry. I will never forget Pastor Ron's reaction when he read the prologue! You guys are the best!

To God be the glory!

Prologue

Gelina pressed back against the storefront, scanning the unfamiliar street. It looked safe. She stepped out of the shadow, her stiletto heels clicking against the concrete as she ran to the curb and dashed across the connecting road.

From the side street the low, powerful hum of a geared-down motor sounded.

She hadn't lost them!

Her heart lurched violently in her chest, pumping terror through her veins. She broke into a dead run down the deserted sidewalk toward a patch of darkness under a broken streetlight.

Maybe I should throw my purse into the middle of the road. Maybe he'll stop looking for me if I give him the money!

Light from the oncoming car pierced the night, spreading in an ever widening swath across the pavement behind her as it approached. She had to hide. But where?

The deeper darkness of a recessed doorway appeared on her left. Gelina darted up the short flight of stairs, then wedged back against the side wall as a long, black car pulled up to the intersection. The black fishnet stockings stretched across her thighs caught on the building's rough stones.

Where to go? Tony won't be satisfied until he makes an example of me. If he finds me, he'll kill me just to show the other girls, she thought frantically.

A sob caught in Gelina's throat, choking off her air. She leaned her head back against the stones and closed her eyes. *Oh, God! Oh, God! If You're real, help me. Help me!*

White light from the car's headlamps swept across her eyelids. They were turning in her direction. She was trapped! Fear writhed like a living thing in her stomach.

The car started a slow crawl down the street toward her.

No! Oh, God, no! I don't want to die!

With a spasmodic jerk, Gelina spun around and grabbed the knob on one of the double doors beside her. Her clammy hands slipped on the cold, polished brass. Locked!

The hum of the car motor grew louder. Her heart bucked like a wild thing. She grabbed the other knob and gave it a violent twist. The latch clicked back as the gleam of the headlights threw her shadow against the painted wood. At that moment, she yanked the door open and leaped inside the building. She slammed the door closed and collapsed against it, her chest heaving with silent sobs.

The hum of the powerful motor faded away down the street.

"Good evening."

Gelina jerked upright and spun about.

"I'm afraid the service has already started. But better late than never." An elderly man smiled and handed her a leaflet. In the center of the cover was a large cross with the word Crossroads emblazoned on the horizontal bar.

Hysterical laughter bubbled up into Gelina's throat. She was in a church. Of all places! Tony would never—

"We're quite crowded because of our guest speaker, but if you'll just come this way, I'll have one of the ushers seat you."

The hysterical laughter died. Gelina stared at the man. Was he blind? Any fool could see she didn't belong in a church. Her long, brassy-blond hair swung side to side as she shook her head. "No, thank you. I'll just wait here a moment."

The hum of that powerful motor sounded nearer. A car door slammed. Gelina dropped the leaflet and whirled to face the door. She jumped when the man touched her arm.

"You're in trouble, aren't you?"

Mute with terror, she nodded.

The man gave her a little push as footsteps approached the door. "Go through those doors. *Hurry!*"

She stumbled forward, caught her balance and ran.

"…so there's no need to be afraid, no matter what your situation or circumstance. Our God is a big God.

He's King of Kings, and Lord of Lords. The great I Am. He watches over His children to care for them, to protect them. But I don't expect you to take my word for it. God Himself tells us in His word.''

The preacher's words seemed to fill the room. Gelina took the church bulletin a smiling usher handed her, slid into an empty spot in the back pew on the right and glanced over her shoulder at the double doors. They remained closed. She clasped the bulletin and her gold shoulder bag in her trembling hands, took a long, deep breath to calm herself, and looked around for another exit.

''Look at Psalm ninety one, verse three. 'For he will deliver you from the snare of the fowler.' Verse five; 'You will not fear the terror of the night, or the destruction that wastes at noonday.'''

Gelina snapped her gaze to the tall, blond young man standing in the pulpit. His head lifted. He looked out over the congregation.

''And just look at the promises God makes in verses fourteen, fifteen and sixteen.'' He began to quote by heart. '''Those who love me, I will deliver; I will protect those who know my name.''' His gaze slid over Gelina—came back and held her own gaze captive. '''When they call to me, I will answer them; I will be with them in trouble.'''

Gelina stiffened. Her long, scarlet nails poked holes through the bulletin and dug into the gold purse. Was he talking to *her?* No. That was foolishness.

'''I will rescue them and honor them. With long life I will satisfy them, and show them my salvation.'''

Nonetheless, Gelina sagged with relief when the pastor's gaze shifted, swept over the people.

"Who are these promises for? They're for those who love God, who know His name. They are for His children. For those who walk in close, personal relationship with Him."

The pastor placed both hands on the pulpit and leaned forward. "Are *you* a child of God? Do *you* have a personal relationship with Jesus Christ?" His gaze swept over the congregation again. "If not—all you have to do is ask. God's salvation is available to all. He loves us." His gaze slid back to Gelina. "He loves *you.*"

The softly spoken words shot like an arrow straight to her heart. Tears welled into her eyes and spilled over. She couldn't stop them, couldn't pull her gaze from the young pastor's face as he stepped out from behind the pulpit and descended the few steps to the center aisle.

"If you don't know how to ask, come forward and I'll pray with you. Just come forward—we'll ask Him together."

Gelina couldn't breathe. She reached down and gripped the hard seat of the wooden pew fighting an inner urge so strong she shook with the force of it. She bit down hard on her lower lip to stop the sobs clawing their way into her throat, and looked down at her lap, horribly ashamed of what she was—of how she looked.

She drew a shuddering breath and tugged at the black leather miniskirt she wore trying to cover her slender thighs. She couldn't go forward. God wouldn't want her. She was too dirty, too shamed, too—

"He *loves* you! Just as you are…Jesus loves you."

The words rang through the room.

Gelina jerked her head up and met the pastor's steady gaze.

"Just as you are."

The quiet words were accompanied by a feeling of warmth, of well-being that Gelina had never known. Wave after wave of it washed over her. God *loved* her. He knew what she was, and He still loved her! Somehow, someway, deep down inside, she knew it was true. She could feel it. She could *feel* God's love for her.

Suddenly, everything inside her went still. Gelina drew a long, deep breath and closed her eyes as the despair and terror that had filled her were swept away by a peace she could not understand.

Awed by the sudden certainty of a Heavenly Father that loved her, that *cared* about her, she gripped the back of the pew in front of her and rose to her feet. The open church bulletin fluttered down, covering the gold shoulder bag that slid off her lap and fell, unheeded, to the floor. She drew another steadying breath, stepped into the aisle and walked forward.

The gold-and-diamond rings on Tony's hands glittered as he shoved the swinging doors open, stepped into the sanctuary and swept a searching gaze over the pews full of people. There was no leather-garbed blonde in sight. Cursing under his breath, he moved toward the empty spot in the pew on the right to get a better view.

If Gelina had gotten away because of that talkative old fool in the vestibule... His foot brushed against something on the floor as he stepped into the pew. He glanced down—there was a church bulletin covering some woman's purse.

Stupid woman! Tony drew his lips back in a sneer, sat down and reached for the purse. He froze as the old man that had followed him into the sanctuary stepped to the end of the pew and shook his head.

Tony threw the man an ugly look, then rose to his feet and again scanned the assemblage. There was no sign of Gelina. She wasn't there—unless she was the one that circle of people up front were praying over.

He snickered at the thought, gave the purse a vicious, satisfying kick, then shoved past the old man and left the sanctuary.

Angela pulled the new, cream-colored turtleneck shirt over her head and glanced around the lovely bedroom. Two nights she had slept here. Two nights she had been safe from the terror that had threatened her every night since her mother and stepfather had forced her into prostitution to pay for their drug habits.

She broke off the thought, snipped the tag from her new, brown wool pants and pulled them on. That life was behind her now—if she could escape the city. Her stomach knotted. She had stayed hidden in this house yesterday, but she didn't fool herself that Tony had given up the search. He couldn't afford to let her get away.

Angela shivered, and sat down to lace on her new shoes. If only they would deliver her car, she could be gone before Tony woke up and hit the streets looking for her. She glanced toward the small alarm clock on the nightstand and her gaze skimmed across the Bible resting there. A frown creased her forehead. Should she ask God to help her escape? Would God *do* that?

Angela bit down on her lower lip, shot a quick look at the closed door, then shut her eyes. "God, if that pastor was right, and this is the sort of thing You do— would You please help me to escape Tony? I need to get out of town so I can start a new life. Thank You."

Heat climbed into Angela's cheeks. She must be crazy, asking God for help. She never asked *anyone* for help. It had been just her against the world for as long as she could remember.

She shrugged off the odd feeling, tucked in the turtleneck, fastened the belt of the slacks and reached for the matching plaid blazer. Her movement, reflected in the full-length mirror hanging on the open closet door, caught her attention. For a long moment she stared at the young, slender woman looking back at her.

Born again.

The phrase the young pastor had used popped into her mind. Angela smiled, then leaned forward and stared hard at her reflection. Her smile was different. There was less brittleness, less of an edge. And her eyes looked softer…warmer.

She stepped closer and lifted her hand to touch the young woman in the mirror. The reflected fingertips met hers and a sense of wonder filled her. It was really her. A *new* her.

"Hello, Angela." The brown, heavily fringed eyes staring back at her from the mirror widened in surprise. Even her voice sounded different. It sounded... gentle. How had these things happened? She started at a soft rapping on the door.

"Miss Warren?"

"Just a moment."

Angela slipped on the blazer, took one last awed look at her reflection and turned toward the door. Her gaze fell on the tube of bright-red lipstick sitting on top of the dresser among the crimson blush and other items of makeup. With one quick swipe of her hands she picked it all up and tossed it into the wastebasket. It landed on top of the gold purse, black-leather mini-skirt, net stockings and other garish items of clothing covered with cutoff tresses of long, brassy-blond hair.

Angela brushed her hands together in satisfaction, turned her back on the wastebasket that held all that remained of Gelina, and opened the bedroom door.

"Yes, Mrs. Parker?"

"I just wanted to let you know your car has been delivered. It's in the—" The woman stopped and stared.

"Surprised, Mrs. Parker?"

"Surprised? I'm astounded." The elderly woman pursed her lips and made a slow circle around Angela. "My, my! I've seen transformations before, but this is...well...it's astonishing."

The woman laughed at her own reaction and reached up to touch one of the soft, silky wisps of brown hair framing Angela's face. "I love your hair. That short style is perfect on you. And the color is wonderful."

Angela smiled. "The credit is yours, Mrs. Parker. You picked it out."

The woman laughed again. "That's true. I did. But I only bought what you asked for." She swept her gaze over Angela's slender body and nodded in obvious satisfaction. "The clothes fit well." She looked down at the suede pant boots. "Are the shoes all right?"

"They fit fine. Everything fits. I can't thank you enough for going to all this trouble for me."

Angela reached for the new brown leather purse on the dresser. "If you'll let me know what I owe you for the room and the shopping…for arranging for your hair stylist to come, and all the rest of your help, I'll pay—"

"Hush." Angela glanced down at the hand Nora Parker placed on her arm. "It was no trouble, dear. It was a pleasure. I'm glad Pastor Barnes suggested me to the visiting pastor when he asked for people who would be willing to help you. There's no charge."

"But—"

Nora Parker smiled and shook her head.

Angela suddenly felt extremely awkward. What should she do? No one had ever done anything to help her without expecting payment.

"Would it make you feel better to pay, dear?"

Ah! Angela's face tightened. She was back on familiar territory now. She knew this game. A sudden sense of disappointment filled her. She ignored it and nodded agreement. "Name your price, Mrs. Parker. I won't quibble." She reached into her purse for money. Nora Parker stayed her hand. She looked up and met the elderly woman's gaze.

"If someday you meet a young woman in trouble...you help her in my name. That's the payment I want, dear."

Angela was so shocked, she barely felt the gentle squeeze the elderly woman gave her hand before she left the room.

Elaine Madison's Home for Abused Women and Children. Angela copied the address out of the telephone book onto the stamped envelope, signed Nora Parker's name to the card, then slipped it and the money orders she'd bought inside and dropped the envelope in the local mail slot on her way out of the post office. The first installment on her debt to Mrs. Parker had been paid. It would never be enough.

She hurried across the parking lot, unlocked her new car, then pulled the map she needed first from her travel bag and backed out of the parking place. When the light at the corner stopped traffic, she exited the parking lot onto Oakwood Boulevard and headed north.

What a beautiful morning! Beautiful, but chilly for early September. Angela pulled up behind a green van stopped for the red light at Trenton Street and leaned forward to adjust the heater. She would have to include a coat when she stopped to buy her new wardrobe. And maybe one of those fleece jackets she'd been seeing everywhere.

A long, black car rolled to a halt beside her.

Angela's stomach contracted sharply. *Tony!* What was he doing on the streets before late afternoon? Bile surged into her throat. She knew the answer—he was hunting for her. She reached down and pushed the button that locked all the doors, then gripped the steering wheel with her trembling hands and stared straight ahead.

Out of the corner of her eye she could see Tony staring at her. He said something to the man driving the car. The driver turned his head to look at her and both men laughed. Angela's heart gave a painful jolt. She stared at the back of the van ahead of her.

God, please—please! Make it move!

The light turned green. Angela let out her breath and moved ahead with the traffic. If only she could pass! But there was no chance; oncoming traffic blocked her on the left, and Tony's car pinned her in on the right.

Her head began to throb. Suddenly, Tony's car leaped ahead. She watched in utter amazement as it exited onto the Baker Street Bridge and headed back toward the main part of the city.

He hadn't recognized her. Tony hadn't recognized her! She was free. Angela sagged back against the seat, sobbing and laughing.

The flash of her exit sign sobered her. She took a deep breath, accelerated up the on-ramp and headed west toward her new life.

Chapter One

"**H**ello, the house!"

Angela smiled at the familiar call. "I'm in the library, Leigh."

"Where else?" The sound of footsteps approached down the hallway. A shiny curtain of smooth red hair swung into Angela's view as Leigh Roberts stuck her head around the door casing. "You don't look ready to leave for the welcome dinner at church. How much longer will you be?"

Angela stopped typing and smiled at her best friend. "Give me ten more minutes."

"That's cutting it pretty close. I want to make a good impression on the new pastor, and so should you." Leigh waggled her eyebrows. "He's young and single, you know. And I hear he's a hunk."

Angela laughed. "*I'm* supposed to be the information expert. I swear, Leigh, if I had your sources I'd be a millionaire."

"No doubt." Leigh grinned, then gave an audible sniff. "What is that divine smell?"

"I'm experimenting with a new cinnamon syrup to pour on the apple pies they asked me to bake for the welcome dinner. Have a taste. I'll be right along." Angela waved her friend off to the kitchen and turned back to her computer.

"There he is." Leigh's green eyes widened. "Wow! He *is* a hunk."

Laughing at her friend's enthusiastic, under-her-breath comment, Angela turned to follow the direction of Leigh's appreciative gaze and found herself looking straight into her past. It was so unexpected she could only stare as her past and present walked toward her in the form of their new, tall, blond pastor.

"Angela? What's wrong?"

Leigh's sudden grip on her arm broke the numbing paralysis of the shock. Angela shook her head. "Nothing." She had to get out of there before he saw her! If she could reach the back door—

"Nothing?" Leigh stared at her friend. "You're as white as that little lie you just told me." She pulled a chair forward. "Sit down before you pass out. I'll go get you some water, unless—" Her eyes narrowed as she studied Angela's face. "Are you going to be ill? Do you need me to help you to the ladies' room?"

The ladies' room! She would be safe there until she could think what to do. Angela shot Leigh a look of gratitude and shook her head. "No, thanks. I can make it on my own. You stay here. I'll—"

"Ladies, I'd like you to meet our new pastor."

Too late! Angela's stomach heaved. *Lord, don't let me be sick.* She drew a long, deep breath, rose to her feet and turned around as Walter Foster, one of the elders of the church, continued his introduction.

"Pastor Stevens, this is Leigh Roberts and Angela Warren. They are in charge of special activities. If you need someone to come up with interesting ideas for outings, make unusual and beautiful decorations, or research a missionary project these are the women you call on."

Hosea Stevens smiled. "I'll keep that in mind." He reached for Leigh's extended hand. "Do I address you as Miss or Mrs. Roberts? Or do you prefer Ms.?"

Leigh laughed. "Ms. is too generic a term for my liking, Pastor Stevens. And I'm not a Mrs. for a few months yet. Actually, it's Dr. Roberts. But that's too formal. Call me Leigh—everyone does."

"Then Leigh it is." The pastor gave her another smile and turned to take Angela's offered hand.

"And you, Angela Warren?" His gaze skimmed over her face. "Are you married or modern or—?"

"It's Miss Warren, Pastor Stevens. I'm not married, or modern." His strong fingers curled more tightly around her hand.

"You're shaking, Miss Warren. And your hand is like ice. Are you ill?"

There was genuine concern in his voice. Angela's eyes filled. It had been six years, but she remembered that concern. She shook her head and looked down at their joined hands. *Father God, please—make him let go of my hand. Help me to get out of here!* She gave a little tug and Pastor Stevens released her hand.

"You *are* pale, Angela." Walter Foster stepped closer and laid a fatherly hand on her shoulder. "Maybe you should take her home, Leigh."

"No! I—I mean, no…please." The last thing she wanted was Leigh fussing over her and asking her questions. Angela forced a smile. "There's no reason for Leigh to miss the meeting. I'm perfectly capable of taking myself home."

She didn't dare look at Hosea Stevens. Instead, she grabbed the purse she'd laid on the table and turned toward her friend. "Leigh, can you—?"

"Don't worry about me, Angela. Barbara Adams can drop me off at your place to pick up my car." Leigh's voice took on its professional tone as she studied Angela's face. "Are you certain you're able to drive home?"

Angela nodded her head. "I'll be fine. And I'll expect a full report on the meeting in the morning." She opened her purse and searched for her car keys as an excuse not to have to look at the men. "Now, if you'll all excuse me—" She jumped as Leigh's hand touched her forehead.

"You don't have a fever, Angela, but still, I think you must have picked up that summer flu bug that's going around. Drink lots of liquids, and go straight to bed. And if you need anything, call me. Otherwise, I'll check on you tomorrow, I won't wake you when I get the car."

Angela nodded and turned toward the exit.

"I hope you feel better soon, Miss Warren. We'll remember you in our prayers."

Angela paused with her hand on the push bar of the

glass door and glanced back over her shoulder. "Thank you, Pastor Stevens." A shiver ran through her as their gazes touched. Quickly, she pushed the door open, stepped out into the warm summer evening and hurried to her car.

The keys in Angela's hand jingled as another nervous tremor shook her body. She stared down at them, frowned, then slowly lifted her head and swept a startled gaze around her bedroom. She didn't remember driving home.

Dropping the keys onto her dresser, she hurried to the dormer windows and yanked the curtains closed. Even here, in the place that had been her home for the last six years, she felt exposed. Was there no place she could be safe from the past?

Angela turned and threw herself onto the bed as the pain in her heart swelled and spread. She had worked so hard to leave her past behind. No one in the town of Harmony knew about her—no one—until now.

Oh, why had Pastor Hosea Stevens come here?

A sob erupted from Angela's throat into the quiet of the room. She buried her face in her pillow as the tears began to flow.

"Hello?"

"Angela! Finally! If that machine had answered one more time I was going to get in the car and drive over there."

"Hello, Leigh."

"Hi. Sorry about that tirade, but this is the third

time I've called, and I was getting worried. How are you feeling?''

"Terrible." Angela rolled over onto her back and covered her swollen, burning eyes with her free arm.

"I'm not surprised. I've never seen the flu hit anyone so hard or fast. I thought you were going to faint." There was a significant pause. "Our new pastor seemed quite concerned about you."

Oh, no! Angela bolted to a sitting position. She could almost hear Leigh's eyebrows waggling over the phone, and the last thing she needed was for her friend to start playing matchmaker.

"No comment, eh? All right. All right. Your silence is shouting at me. We'll discuss Pastor Stevens another time. Is there anything you need? Chicken soup or something?" Leigh's low laughter came floating over the wire. "Not that I can make any. But I can run to the store and buy you some."

Angela sank back down onto her pillow and covered her eyes. Her head was spinning from her sudden movement. "Thanks, Leigh, but I'm fine for now."

"Okay. I'll hang up so you can rest. But if you're not better by tomorrow I'm paying you a professional visit after church. Even OBs know how to treat the flu. Oops—I'm being paged. Call if you need me. Bye."

Church? Tomorrow was Sunday! Angela's stomach churned. She slammed the receiver down and ran for the bathroom. What was she to do about church? What was she to do about her life?

She reached the bathroom just in time.

* * *

The teakettle whistled.

Angela read the Bible verses one more time, then went to make her tea as she pondered them. "Trust in the Lord with all your heart, and lean not on your own understanding. In all your ways acknowledge Him, and He will make your paths straight."

The words were comforting, but were they her answer? Angela carried her tea back to the table and read the verses again. They would certainly apply to—

The sharp ring of the telephone made her jump. She started toward the counter to pick up the receiver, then stopped. What if it was him? She held her breath, waiting for the answering machine to click on.

"Miss Warren? This is Pastor Stevens. I'm calling to see how you're feeling."

Hosea Stevens's deep, rich voice filled the small kitchen.

"I hope the fact that your machine has answered means you are up and about. But until I know for certain I will keep you in my prayers."

No! She didn't want him thinking about her.

"By the way, I understand I have you to thank for the delicious apple pie. That cinnamon syrup was wonderful! I'd move halfway across the country for a treat like that anytime." There was a low, soft chuckle. "Don't tell my mother, though, she prides herself on her baking." The machine clicked off.

Angela took a deep breath and glanced down at her Bible on the table. "Trust in the Lord with all your heart...."

The words seemed to leap off the page at her. For

a long moment she stood staring down at them; then, slowly, she sank down onto the chair. She did trust the Lord—but Pastor Hosea Stevens was another matter. One word from him about her past, and her life in Harmony would be ruined. Leigh and the other friends she had made would certainly shun her. She hadn't the strength or courage to face that. She would have to move and start again.

Tears filled Angela's eyes. Things had been going so well. Was she to be punished all her life for her past sin? She crossed her arms over the Bible and hid her face against them, consumed by shame.

"Lord, I know I deserve whatever happens. But I'm so sorry for the things I've done. And I know I've asked You many times before, but I ask You again to forgive me. Oh, Lord, please forgive me. And help me, Lord. Help me to trust You for the answer to this situation. I ask it in Your precious, holy name. Amen."

Angela drew a deep breath and rose to her feet. There was a scripture in the book of James that said something about faith without works being dead—she didn't want to be guilty of that. She was going to have to do something tangible to prove she trusted the Lord.

With a sigh that came all the way from her toes, Angela closed her Bible, picked up her cup of tea, and, against all her own instinct and desire, headed for the bedroom to select the outfit she would wear to church tomorrow.

"Wow! He looks like a dream, and preaches like a house afire." Leigh clapped her hand over her heart and rolled her eyes toward heaven. "I think I'm in love!"

Nervous as she was, Angela couldn't help but smile at her friend's outrageous enthusiasm. "Better not let your fiancé hear you say that." She glanced over her shoulder at them both as she filed out of the row.

Leigh laughed and followed her. "Phil understands. Don't you, Phil?" She grinned at the exaggerated growl of agreement from her intended, put her hand on Angela's shoulder and tugged. "Hey, what's the big rush? I'm knocking into people here." She smiled down at the older woman beside her. "Sorry, Mrs. Boyer."

Angela slowed her steps, then had to stop entirely for a toddler that escaped his mother's grasp and darted in front of her. People closed in around her. She'd never seen the church so crowded. Had the entire membership turned out to hear the new pastor preach his first sermon?

She raised up on tiptoe to scan the crowd for a less congested pathway to the door and her heart sank. There was no reason to hurry now—Hosea Stevens was already at the front doors shaking hands. How had he made it through the press of people so quickly?

Angela frowned, and darted a glance toward the side exits. Maybe she could avoid him that way. An elbow jabbed into her ribs. She sighed. It was no use—she would never be able to reach those doors through the crush of people. She took a firmer grip on her Bible and inched her way forward with the crowd.

"Miss Warren!" Hosea Stevens smiled and reached for her hand. "I'm so pleased you are feeling well

enough to attend this morning's service. Are you fully
recovered?''

"Not fully, Pastor Stevens, but with the Lord's help
I will be.''

"Amen to that. The Lord never fails. And you,
Leigh—'' Hosea released her hand and turned toward
her friend. "I'm happy to see you....''

Their voices faded away as Angela stepped through
the open door and almost danced her way down the
stairs to the sidewalk. He didn't recognize her! She
had been worrying over nothing.

"Angela. Wait a minute!'' Leigh dodged around an
elderly couple on the sidewalk and hurried toward her.
"Phil and I are going to Romans for lunch with Patty
and Doug and we want you to come.''

Angela looked over at the people waiting for Leigh
by Phil's car. "I don't think so, Leigh. I'd be a fifth
wheel and—''

"Angela Warren, you know none of us feel like
that! Now, come on, it'll be fun.'' Leigh linked her
arm through Angela's and started back toward the others. "But...if you're serious about that fifth wheel
thing, I could invite Phil's brother Bob.''

Angela dug in her heels and Leigh almost tripped.
She heaved a sigh. "Oh, all right—no men for you.''

"Promise?''

"I promise. But I still don't see what you have
against them.'' Leigh brushed a long lock of red hair
back out of her eyes and started walking again.
"Every single man in this church between the ages
of—no, just make that every single man in this
church—is crazy about you, Angela. And you won't

give any of them a chance. I don't get it.'' She gave her a sidelong look. "Some of them are really nice.''

"I know they are, Leigh.'' Angela met Leigh's gaze. "We've been over this before. I just don't want any romantic involvement with anyone. I like my life the way it is. Okay?''

"Okay.'' Leigh lifted her mouth in a roguish grin. "But you may not have any say in the matter.''

Angela stopped walking and stared up at her. "What does that mean? What are you talking about?''

Leigh's grin grew wider. "I've been praying for you. That's what I'm talking about. Now come on.'' She linked her arm through Angela's and tugged. "Phil made reservations for one o'clock and I don't want to lose our table—I'm starving!''

Chapter Two

❧

"**B**all one!"

"Way to go, Angela! That's the way to read 'em."

Angela swept off her ball cap, bowed to Leigh who was taking a long lead off first base, then replaced her cap and tugged it low to hide her face. Her gaze lifted to the man on the pitcher's mound. So much for hiding in the crowd at the church picnic. She should never have come. Four weeks since his arrival, and she was still a nervous wreck. She tugged the cap lower and lifted the bat into position.

Hosea Stevens wound up and pitched the ball.

"Strrrike one!"

Leigh scurried back to first as Phil caught the pitch and threw it to Seth Pickard.

"You've got to be faster than that, Phil, this woman of yours runs like a deer!" Leigh waggled her eyebrows at him. Seth laughed, and threw the ball to Hosea.

Leigh inched off base again.

Hosea wound up and pitched it right down the middle.

Crack!

Leigh let out a whoop, and took off running as Angela dropped the bat and dashed for first base.

The ball whizzed out to center field. Bill Stoner scooped it up and threw to Lou Harris at third base. Leigh skidded to a halt, spun around, dashed back to second base, grinned and gave Angela, who had returned to first, a thumbs-up. "Good hit!"

"Thanks." Angela drew a deep breath and glanced toward home plate. "Come on, Debby, hit us in!" Please hit us in, she begged silently. I want out of here! Her gaze shifted to Hosea Stevens as he began his windup. She pulled her thoughts back to the business at hand and inched her way off base.

Hosea pitched another perfect strike.

Crack!

Debby popped it up, and Angela took off for second base.

Hosea faded back, leaped into the air, caught the ball for out number one, threw it to Lou Harris at third, who tagged a laughing, dodging Leigh for out number two, and threw it to Bart Williams at second.

Angela skidded to a halt, let out a squeal, and spun around to head back to first. She froze in place. Hosea Stevens was standing not ten feet away between her and first base. He caught the ball Bart lobbed to him, grinned, and started a slow advance toward her. She backed up. Hosea's grin widened. He locked his gaze on hers and took another step toward her. Her stomach jittered.

Not him, Lord. Please, not him!

Angela shoved her hands out toward Hosea, palms foremost, took another step backward, then spun about and almost crashed into Bart who had sneaked up behind her.

Bart laughed, caught the ball Hosea tossed him and tapped Angela lightly on her shoulder. "Whooeee… triple play! That's the game, folks! Let's go eat!"

"Great game, Slider." Bart slapped Hosea on the shoulder and trotted off to join the rest of the players that were headed toward the shaded tables under the pavilions along the river.

"Slider?" Leigh stopped beside Angela and gaped at Hosea. "You're *Slider Stevens?*"

"I used to be."

"Well, no wonder we lost!"

Hosea laughed.

Phil draped his arm around Leigh's shoulders and dropped a kiss on top of her head. "That's my little competitor talking, Pastor." He laughed down at Leigh. "He went easy on you, sweetheart. Do you think any of you would have gotten a hit if he hadn't?"

"Judas! You should have told me." Leigh aimed a playful punch at Phil's stomach. He caught her hand and kissed it.

Angela smiled at their antics and glanced at Hosea. "I guess I missed something. I don't understand the significance of Slider Stevens."

His gaze met hers. "That's because it has no significance, now. It's just a name out of my past. I picked it up when I played college ball.''

"Oh." Angela's composure unraveled. Had he remembered *her* other name?

Leigh gave a disdainful snort and ducked out from under Phil's arm. "'Played college ball'—hah! That's an understatement. He was the best, Angela. Don't you remember all that publicity when he was being wooed by the major league teams?"

Angela shook her head and turned away, too distracted by her thoughts to take part in the conversation.

"Well, I sure do." Phil looked at Hosea. "You were offered a huge contract, but you never signed. I always wondered why someone with your talent gave up such a fantastic chance."

"Well, wonder no more. There's a very simple answer." Hosea scooped up a ball someone had dropped and stepped over to toss it into a basket full of equipment. "God had a different plan for my life—I went to Bible college."

"And gave up all those *millions?* Not to mention the fame, and the adulation of baseball fans everywhere."

Phil's incredulous tone penetrated Angela's preoccupation. She glanced over at Hosea Stevens. Had he done that?

Hosea pulled off his cap and scrubbed his hand through his hair. "I gained far more than I gave up, Phil. It was the best decision I've ever made. I gained riches beyond value." He tugged his cap back on. "Now…I think Bart had the right idea. I know I've worked up a healthy appetite. Anyone care to join me at the picnic table?''

"Sounds good to me."

Phil laughed and draped his arm around Leigh again. "Food always sounds good to you, my sweet."

"True." She grinned up at him. "But, I happen to know Angela brought her famous potato salad, *and* her even more famous strawberry shortcake."

Phil rolled his eyes and licked his lips. "Say no more—let's go!" He slid his hand down to catch hold of Leigh's and took off at a dead run toward the tables.

Hosea laughed. "I guess they're hungry."

They were alone! Angela forced a smile. "Yes. Hungry and energetic." She started walking toward the tables. There was safety in numbers, and if she could just reach the crowd she could get away from him.

"Famous potato salad, and even more famous strawberry shortcake, huh? I've got to have some of that."

Angela's nerves tingled as Hosea fell into step beside her. She wiped her moist palms against her khaki shorts and stared down at the grass. "Then you'd better know, Pastor Stevens, that 'famous' is an exaggeration."

"I hope not, Miss Warren. But, to be honest, it probably wouldn't matter at this point. I'm hungry as a bear coming out of hibernation."

Angela glanced up at him from beneath the brim of her baseball cap and her stomach went all jittery again. She jerked her gaze away from his face and took a deep breath. "Excuse me, Pastor Stevens, I have to get the whipped cream from my car."

Veering off to the right, she headed for the parking lot to compose herself. She could feel his gaze following her all the way.

Millions of dollars. Had he really given up millions of dollars?

Angela leaned against a tree, sipped her iced tea and watched Hosea Stevens laugh, talk and hand out roasted corn to all comers. He couldn't be more alien to her if he had suddenly grown fur and a tail. Her stepfather and Tony would have killed for that much money. It was inconceivable to her that this man had willingly given it up to obey the Lord.

Angela frowned and studied Hosea Stevens's face. What had he answered Phil?...*I gained riches beyond value.* Did he truly mean that?

"What are you looking so serious, about? Don't you know this is a picnic?"

Angela jumped and looked up at Alan Curtis, another church member. He smiled down at her.

"Sorry, I didn't mean to startle you. But you looked so solemn—and at least a thousand miles away."

"No, I'm right here." Angela gave him a polite smile and pushed away from the tree. "And now, I'm going over there, and try a piece of that coconut cake Emily brought. It looks wonderful." She headed toward the dessert table.

"I don't know about the cake—but I can highly recommend the strawberry shortcake." Alan turned to walk beside her. "What do you do to those biscuits?"

''Ah, that's a secret.''

''Well it's a secret worth money.'' He smiled again. ''You could probably sell the recipe to one of those famous chefs for big bucks.''

''Why, thank you, sir.''

Big bucks. Millions of dollars. Angela lifted her gaze beyond Alan to the bonfire where the corn was roasting—to where Hosea was pulling back the shucks and handing it out to the laughing, chatting members of his congregation. No man willingly gave up millions of dollars. There had to be a reason.

She turned back to the table and gave Alan an absent smile as he handed her a piece of the coconut cake. She would find that reason when she got home. As she'd reminded Leigh, information was her specialty. For now, she'd stay hidden in the crowd at the table. She picked up a napkin and plastic fork and took a seat.

''Come on, Angela! They're lining up for the water balloon toss, and we need another woman.''

Angela sighed and gave up as Leigh grabbed her hand and tugged her to her feet. There was just no way she could stay lost in the crowd with Leigh around.

''There's Phil.'' Leigh waved her free hand through the air to catch his attention as they trotted forward. ''Here we are!''

Angela's heart sank as she spotted Hosea Stevens lined up beside Phil on the other side of the open field. *Leigh*. This had her matchmaking fingerprints all over it. She stopped short. ''Leigh, I don't—'' The shrill blow of a whistle cut off her protest. Leigh tugged her into place on the line.

"Well…now that we're all here." Walter Foster looked pointedly at Leigh and laughed when she grinned and curtsied to him. "Let's begin." He glanced around. "You all know the rules. You throw the balloon to your partner. When everyone has thrown their balloon, I'll blow my whistle and you all take a step backward before your partner throws it back to you. You're out of the contest as soon as your balloon breaks. Okay?"

There was a chorus of agreement.

"All right. Men…hold up your balloons! Ladies…check the color of your partner's balloon. We've separated them so if somebody throws a wild one at you you'll know in time to dodge it!" He glanced around to make sure everyone was ready while people laughed and shouted threats at one another. "Okay, last couple on the field wins all the extra balloons!"

He waved the half-empty bag over his head and hurried out of the cleared area to the accompaniment of the good-natured insults called out at the offered prize. When he reached the safety of the sidelines he turned and lifted his hand. Everyone quieted and looked at their partner.

"Ready…set…*Go!*"

Two dozen multicolored balloons wobbled through the air.

Angela caught the blue one Hosea threw to her, instinctively drawing her hands down and backward to ease the contact.

There was a sharp squeal to Leigh's left. Another farther down the line.

Cold water spattered Angela's sun-warmed legs as a balloon burst on the ground beside her. She jumped.

"Sorry, Angela, you got more of that than I did." Sandra Collins laughed and trotted off the field with the other women whose balloons had broken.

The whistle blew. The remaining players took a step back.

Angela judged the new distance and threw the balloon to Hosea. Water splashed everywhere as wildly thrown balloons broke and spewed their contents on whoever happened to be in the way.

Hosea caught hers, then burst into laughter as another smacked against his shoulder and sprayed him with water. He held the dripping remnant of the wayward balloon out to Lou Harris. "I believe this belongs to you, sir?"

Lou accepted it with a bow.

The crowd laughed.

The whistle blew.

Angela stepped back. Hosea looked at her over the widening space. Thank goodness they were moving farther apart. She felt naked without the baseball cap. *Lord, don't let him remember. Please—*

Whap!

Angela gasped as the blue balloon broke against her abdomen and cold water soaked through her cotton shirt and khaki shorts. *Idiot! You closed your eyes.* She shook her head at her foolishness, and tugged her wet shirt out away from her body.

"Woo-hoo! Only three more to go and we win,

Phil!'' Leigh looked over at her friend and grinned. ''Sorry, Angela.''

Angela laughed. ''Yeah, I can tell.'' She dropped back out of harm's way and trotted off the field as the whistle sounded again.

Hosea Stevens met her at the edge of the crowd.

She sucked in a breath and pasted a smile on her face. ''I'm sorry, Pastor. I cost you a half bag of balloons.''

He grinned down at her. ''I think I can manage to live through the disappointment.'' His gaze sought hers. ''I'm sorry about the soaking.''

Angela turned away to look back at the field. ''My fault entirely.'' There was a sudden burst of applause. ''Besides, it seems to have worked out well for Leigh and Phil.'' She gave him a quick glance. ''Excuse me, I have to go congratulate them.''

Relieved at the excuse to leave his company, she trotted off to join her friends.

Angela stared at the computer screen. She'd been so eager to check the information on Hosea ''Slider'' Stevens, she hadn't even changed out of her picnic clothes, and she'd found nothing questionable. She checked her files, her sources of information again. There was nothing. No illness, injury or family problems. No breath of scandal or unexplained absences for any block of time. All she could find confirmed Hosea's statement. He had simply walked away from the millions of dollars offered him to play professional ball. And that included a signing bonus in a previously unheard of amount for a rookie.

She shook her head and scanned the copy of the newspaper reports again. There was nothing else to check. Nowhere else to go for information. What he had said was true. But, how could it be? She must have missed something. Men weren't like that.

Angela closed her eyes, rubbed her temples and rotated her neck. Maybe she was just tired. It had been a long day. She'd check things over again tomorrow. She turned off the computer, climbed the stairs and prepared for bed. The softness of the mattress felt lovely after the physical activity of the day. She sighed, and closed her eyes.

"Thank you, Father, for the blessings of this day. Thank you for the lovely weather and the picnic...."

An image of Hosea Stevens's face implanted itself on Angela's mind stopping her words. She popped her eyes open, flopped onto her back and frowned. The man was a torment to her. What was she to do?

"What do You want from me, Lord? What are You after? Why did You bring him here?"

There was no answer to her whispered words. Angela sighed, and turned on the light. The pleasant tiredness of the day was gone. There was only a restless confusion swirling through her brain.

She grabbed her pillows, propped them against the head of the bed and reached for the book she'd left on her nightstand. Reading about the hair-raising adventures of the brooding, dark-haired, brown-eyed espionage agent would not only get her thoughts off her troubles, it would drive the image of the blond, blue-eyed, square-jawed Hosea Stevens out of her mind.

* * *

Hosea flipped his baseball cap onto the shelf, laid his glove beside it and closed the closet door. It had been a fun day. And the church picnic had given him a valuable glimpse of the members of his new congregation in a relaxed setting. He was already learning their individual personalities and quirks. Like Leigh Roberts's love of food. He grinned, stripped off his clothes and tossed them in the laundry basket. The woman ate like a linebacker! How did she stay so thin? Angela Warren on the other hand—she'd merely picked at her food.

Hosea shook his head. He'd tried six years ago to find out what happened to the young woman—if anyone had counseled her after her salvation experience. But when he'd called Pastor Barnes to find out, all the man could tell him was that Angela Warren had left the city. Now, here she was in his church. And judging from what he'd been told and the records he'd seen, she was a valuable, active member. Still, she seemed…uneasy? No. It was something more than that. He just couldn't quite put his finger on it. Did whatever it was have its roots in her past? "Lord, You know what's wrong. Please give me wisdom to help Angela. Amen."

He stood waiting for a moment, but no answer came. "All right, Lord. In Your time." He grabbed a pair of blue-checked boxer shorts from his dresser drawer and trotted to the shower.

Chapter Three

"**W**ell, I think that covers everything." Hosea flipped the cover of his note pad closed and smiled at the group of people seated around the long table in the conference room adjacent to his office. "Thanks to your prayers and talents, the missionary conference should flow smoothly from beginning to end. And that leaves only one thing I want to say."

He rose to his feet, placed his hands on the table and leaned forward as he glanced from person to person. The fear that had tortured her these last few weeks gripped Angela anew when his gaze met hers. She looked away. Had he remembered now? Was he going to tell them about her?

"Sometimes words are inadequate—even for a pastor."

Everyone laughed, but Angela's stomach tightened.

"This is one of those times, because 'thank you' does not begin to express my gratitude for your warm welcome, your openhearted acceptance of me as your pastor, and your understanding and thoughtfulness. It has been your readiness to help me settle in and become acclimated to a new home and church that has made these last few weeks such a smooth and painless transition period. I can't thank you enough. But I can pray for you.''

Out of the corner of her eye Angela saw him straighten and start around the table. He briefly rested his hands on the shoulders of each person as he prayed.

''Father God in heaven, I pray Your richest blessings upon these, Your children. In Your great love and unending mercy, may You meet their every need, withholding no good gift, but extending healing, deliverance, peace, prosperity, and the greatest gift of all, which is the joy of Your presence in their lives. All this I ask in the matchless name of Your Son, Jesus, our Lord and Savior. Amen.''

The meeting was over. She could escape. Under cover of the general stirring and amiable chatter of the others, Angela gathered her things and headed for the door.

''Miss Warren, I'd like a word with you please. If you'll wait a moment, I'll walk you to your car.''

The softly spoken request froze Angela in her tracks. This was it. Her traitorous feet wouldn't move—wouldn't take her out the door to safety. She forced her lips into a smile as the others bid her goodnight and filed out the door.

The sound of a hymn the music team was practicing for Sunday morning poured through the open door. It did nothing to ease Angela's taut nerves. She felt the blood draining from her face as Hosea Stevens walked over to her, but there was nothing she could do to stop it. Six years of her life—gone. She would have to move. Start over somewhere new.

Angela swallowed back a sudden surge of nausea and stared down at the white knuckles on her hands as he stopped in front of her. She couldn't make herself look up at him. She didn't want to read the knowledge of her past in his eyes.

"Have I done something to offend you, Miss Warren?"

"*What?*" Angela jerked her head up. "I mean—no." Had he not remembered? This wasn't about her past after all. Relief made her weak. She put her hand out and gripped the chair beside the open door for support. "Why do you ask?" He glanced down at her hand and she quickly let go of the chair and stepped out into the hallway. He moved to stand beside her.

"I ask because I've noticed you avoid me whenever possible. And when you are forced into my company—such as at the meeting tonight—you seldom look directly at me, or speak to me." His gaze fastened on hers. "And you always hurry off at the first possible moment."

Angela's heart sank—instead of avoiding Hosea Stevens's attention she had drawn it. She looked down at the Bible in her hand and groped frantically for something to say. She couldn't deny the truth.

"If I have said or done anything…"

Angela drew in a deep breath. She couldn't let him believe he had committed some offense against her. The guilt was hers. "Please don't think that, Pastor

Stevens. It's only that I've been…preoccupied lately.''
That certainly was true.

"I see."

There was concern in his voice. Angela lifted her
head and, for the first time, met Hosea Stevens's gaze
fully. The oddest sensation struck her—a sort of tingling warmth that spread through her entire body. Her
eyes widened with shock. She lowered her head so he
wouldn't notice, and started down the hall. He fell into
step beside her.

"I have to say I'm relieved, Miss Warren. I thought
I'd made a horrible mistake.''

She shook her head. "Not at all, Pastor. I'm sorry
if I gave you that impression.'' She made herself look
back up at him. "Please forgive me.''

"Consider it done.'' He lifted his hands, scrubbed
them through his hair, then jammed them into his
pants pockets. "Well, I'm glad that's over with.''

Angela burst into laughter. She couldn't help it. He
looked like a little boy that had been caught out and
by some stroke of luck escaped punishment.

Hosea chuckled. "I hope you won't tell anyone
what a chickenhearted fellow I am.''

Angela hugged her Bible and purse to her chest and
grinned at him. "Never fear, Pastor. Wild horses could
not drag your secret from me.''

Secret! Her steps faltered. She shouldn't have said
secret. What if the word triggered his memory? She
hurried toward the exit door. "Was there anything
more?''

"No.'' Hosea reached for the push bar. "Not unless
I can help you with whatever it is that has been caus-

ing your…preoccupation.'' His voice softened on the word. ''I've had good training, and a lot of experience at counseling. It's part of my job, you know.''

Angela's stomach knotted. She looked down and rearranged the load in her arms. ''That won't be necessary. But thank you anyway, Pastor. Good night.'' She glanced up and their gazes met. That odd sensation hit her again—along with a sudden awareness of Hosea Stevens's exceptional, dark-blond good looks. Quickly, she stepped through the door he held open.

''Good night, Miss Warren.''

There was a soft swish of air as the door closed behind her.

One o'clock! Angela laid her book on the nightstand and turned out the lamp. It did little to help her wakefulness. She threw another disgusted glance at her alarm clock, frowned at the lateness of the hour and turned onto her side. Plumping her feather pillow with her fist, she laid her head down and closed her eyes. An image of Hosea Stevens smiling down at her slid into her mind. She snapped her eyes open, flopped over onto her other side and stared at the moonlight streaming in the window.

What was wrong with her? Why should she be so agitated by a simple smile? Angela threw off the sheet and clicked the lamp back on. She was being ridiculous. Her sleeplessness had nothing to do with Hosea Stevens—she was probably just hungry.

She jammed her feet into her slippers and headed for the kitchen, but nothing in the cupboards looked

appealing. It was indecent of a pastor to be so handsome and charming! But why it should bother her one
way or another was beyond her. She wanted no part
of any man. She had wanted nothing to do with men
ever since her mother and stepfather had—

Angela snatched her mind back from the brink of
that dark abyss and went to the sink for some water.
She had thought she was free of the past. Now, every
time she saw Hosea Stevens it all came rushing back.
And if—*when*—he remembered…

Angela shuddered, set the glass of water on the
counter and walked over to the window. Moonlight
bathed her small backyard with silver radiance but she
was too upset to appreciate the loveliness of the scene.
She had never expected to feel an attraction for a man,
but tonight, when Hosea Stevens had looked at
her…when their gazes had met…

Oh, stop! Angela turned her back on the moonlight
outside the window and went over to drink the water.
Why was she indulging in such romantic nonsense?
That odd feeling was only a momentary aberration.
She was terrified to be around the man, for goodness'
sakes. At any moment he might recall that night when
she had stumbled into the Crossroads Church to get
away from Tony. But still—

Still nothing! Her safety depended on her staying as
distant from the man as possible. She slammed the
door of her mind closed on all thoughts of Hosea Stevens and headed for the library. There was one sure
way to exorcise such foolishness from her mind—
work. Lots and lots of work.

* * *

The image wouldn't go away. He simply could not get it out of his mind. Hosea rubbed his eyes with his knuckles and stared down at the list of scripture references he'd prepared for Sunday's service—all he saw was Angela Warren's face. The problem was, he wasn't sure why.

Was it because, as her pastor, he was concerned over what she had called her preoccupation? Or was it something more basic? Tonight, when their gazes had met he'd felt as if he'd been slammed by a pile driver!

Hosea leaned back in his chair, rested his elbows on the padded arms, and slowly rubbed his chin against the tented fingers of his joined hands. He'd never felt such a strong, instantaneous attraction to a woman. Maybe this was the beginning of love. Maybe this was the answer to his prayers for a woman to cherish and share his life with. He'd been praying for a couple of years now. Was Angela Warren God's answer to those prayers? Could she—an ex-prostitute—be God's choice for him?

Hosea looked down at the Bible on his desk and pursed his lips in contemplation. There was certainly precedent. God had told the prophet Hosea to marry a promiscuous woman as an example of God's love and mercy toward wayward Israel.

"Whoa!" Hosea snapped forward in his chair. "You're letting you're imagination run away with you, buddy! It's *far* too early to be thinking of marriage. And that precedent doesn't apply. Angela is not a promiscuous woman. Her sin has been forgiven by the Lord, remember? It's as if it never happened."

Hosea closed his eyes. It made no difference. Whether his eyes were open or shut, Angela Warren's face was there in his mind—her lovely, smiling face. He blew his breath out in a long gust and opened his eyes. If this was not of God, he had a problem. And if it *was* of God, he still had a problem. He curved his lips into a wry smile. At least he knew where to find the answer. He closed his Bible and rested his hands on top of it.

"Father God, You know my heart. You know my hunger and desire for a woman to love and share my life with. And You know, also, that I would rather be lonely all of my days than make the wrong choice. I choose not to trust in my own feelings, or rely on my own understanding. Therefore, Father, once again, I come to Your throne of grace and say, choose Thou for me. Have Your way, Father. Make Your will known to me, in this, as in all things, that I might obey. And, Father, as her pastor, I ask for Your wisdom and guidance in helping Angela Warren. Her distress is obvious. And if it is rooted in her past as I suspect—if that's the real reason she's been avoiding me—please help her to know she can trust me. I ask it in the precious name of Your Son, Jesus, my Lord and Savior."

There. The first, most important, step in the resolution of his dilemma had been taken—he had placed it in the Lord's hands. Now, all he had to do was stay yielded to God's will. Not always an easy thing to do. But, God's grace was sufficient.

Hosea folded the list of scriptures, tucked it into his Bible, and glanced at his watch. One o'clock—so back home it would be eleven. Good! His parents never went to bed before watching the evening news. He grabbed the phone's handset, punched a memory button and leaned back.

"Hello?"

"Hi, Mom."

"Hosea!" He could hear the happy smile in her voice. "You don't usually call this late." The smile faded away. "Is there something wrong, honey?"

"No. I just wanted to talk." He took a deep breath. "Mom? Do you remember that young prostitute I told you about when I first started preaching?"

"The one at the Crossroads church? The one that was born again?"

"That's the one. She's here. She's an active member of my new church."

"You're kidding! That's wonderful, Hosea! I'm so pleased she's still walking with the Lord." Her laughter danced out of the receiver into his ear. "But how astonishing that the two of you ended up in the same church halfway across the country! It's almost as if—"

Hosea smiled. She'd got it. There was nothing slow about his mom when it came to the things of the Lord or her children.

"So that's why you called."

"Yes. I'm thinking it's pretty incredible to be a coincidence. And I've never felt this way about anyone. She's wonderful. But there is a problem. I think she's still troubled over her past. I need you and Dad to pray about this with me, Mom. I don't want to make a mistake. I need 'ears to hear.'"

Chapter Four

What a gorgeous September day! Angela opened the sunroof, lowered the windows, and, on a sudden, strong impulse, turned onto Hillman Boulevard. It would take her a few blocks out of her way, but the drive along the river with the tree-covered hills beyond would be worth it. She had earned a little relaxation.

She glanced over at her purse and smiled. Combined with what she had already saved, the sizable pay she had received from the Jones-Thomas Manufacturing Firm for her research report would enable her to take that European vacation she'd been promising herself. And the large bonus check they had given her for finishing before the deadline would take care of new clothes.

Angela's smile widened. She could get that lovely, burgundy silk pantsuit she had been admiring, and that delicious sage-green dress with the flowing skirt as well. Pleased at the prospect, she braked at the red light, flicked on her directional signal and followed a blue car, overflowing with children, onto Riverside Parkway. The trunk lid of the car was strapped down over piled-up coolers, lawn chairs and a small rubber raft.

Looks like someone's going on a last picnic before school starts. Angela smiled. What a lovely idea. She glanced toward the river. She hadn't anyone to picnic with, but a walk along the path would be nice. And she had time… Why not? She laughed, pulled into a parking spot and climbed from the car.

A bird in the branches above her chirped loudly, swooped down out of the tree and flew straight at her head. She let out a startled squeal and ducked, then laughed and turned to watch the bird fly away toward the river. It flew directly over a young woman sitting on a park bench a short distance away. The teenager looked dejected—and familiar. One of the teen group at church?

Angela pulled off her sunglasses for a better view. It was Cathy Anders. She started over the grass toward the girl. "Cathy?"

The teenager glanced over her shoulder. Her hands lifted and wiped across her cheeks.

"Cathy, what's wrong?" Angela skimmed an anxious gaze over the girl as she drew near. "Are you hurt?"

"N-no."

Tears shimmered in the girl's eyes. Angela sat down on the bench beside her and reached for her hand. "Well, there's something wrong, Cathy. Why don't you tell me what it is? Maybe I can help."

The girl shook her head and looked down at her lap. "No one can help."

All sorts of dire circumstances flashed through Angela's mind. She took a deep breath and offered a silent prayer for guidance. "I'd like to try, Cathy—if you'll let me."

"Oh, Miss Warren!" The teenager broke into sobs and threw herself into Angela's arms. "My dad found the money I'd saved for college and he took it. My bus ticket, too. He cashed it in and went to Charlie's. Now I can't get there for registration and they're going to give my scholarship to someone else."

"Charlie's? You mean the tavern where they have off-track betting?" The girl's hair brushed against Angela's cheek as she nodded. "Oh, Cathy, I'm so sorry." She tightened her arms around the weeping girl. "Surely, there's something—" Cathy's forehead rolled back and forth against her shoulder.

"No. I called. They need my share of the money by four o'clock today or I lose the scholarship." Cathy took a long, shuddering breath and straightened. "It's no use talking about it, Miss Warren. I don't have the money now. And I can't get there before registration. I can't get there at all without my ticket." She swiped at her streaming eyes with a balled-up tissue in her hand. "Even if I had the money, if I don't register they will close me out of my classes."

Angela took a deep breath to calm a sudden surge of anger. "Let me understand, Cathy. You say your father *found* your money. Were you hiding it from him?"

Shame washed over the teenager's face. She nodded

and looked away. "I had a savings account where I banked whatever I could save from my pay after I bought food and stuff. But I had to withdraw the money yesterday so I could buy my ticket and be ready to leave early this morning. I hid it in the bag of books I'm…was…taking with me, and he found it."

Fresh tears flowed down Cathy's cheeks. "I know that must sound strange and awful to you, Miss Warren, but—" She glanced at Angela, then looked back down at the wadded tissue in her hands. "But I have to do those things. My dad's a gambler and…and an alcoholic."

"I see." The anger in Angela turned to fury at the pain she saw in the girl's eyes. The anguish of living with an addicted parent wasn't strange to her at all. She knew, far too well, the pain and humiliation Cathy was suffering.

"It's not like you think, Miss Warren." Cathy's back straightened, her chin lifted. "My dad would never have taken my money if it wasn't for the alcohol. That's why I wanted to go to college. I wanted to do medical research." Tears spilled from her eyes again. "Maybe I could have found a way to help people like my dad."

Angela's eyes filled. Her heart ached for Cathy. The denial, and the vehement protection of the parent were all too familiar to her, too. The same insidious emotions had ensnared her until her dreams were dead and her life destroyed. Well, it was too late for her, but it would *not* happen to Cathy! Not if she could help it. Who needed a vacation in Europe anyway?

Unable to restrain herself, Angela gave Cathy a fierce hug, then leaped to her feet. "Come on, Cathy!" She grabbed the astonished teenager by the hand and tugged her off the bench, pulling her along as she ran toward her car.

"What are you doing, Miss Warren? Where are we going?" Cathy's head barely missed the edge of the car roof as Angela all but shoved her into the passenger seat.

"To get you registered for college!" Angela slammed the door behind Cathy, ran around to the driver's side, hopped in, then made a quick U-turn.

Cathy grabbed for the dash and held on. Her tears dried up as they bore down on a dark-green sedan. "You don't understand, Miss Warren. I don't have the money, and—"

"Yes you do, Cathy. I'm going to give it to you."

"What?" The girl's mouth gaped open. She stared in wide-eyed astonishment at Angela. "Why?"

For hundreds of horrible, painful reasons. Angela's hands tightened on the steering wheel as she fought back the dark memories. "Let's just say I'm paying a debt to a lady who once helped me.

"Cathy, it will save time if you'll let me take you home to get your things." Angela frowned as the teenager shook her head.

"I'm sorry, Miss Warren. I know you're trying to help me. And I'm not just being stubborn." Tears swarmed into Cathy's red, swollen eyes. "I know time is important. And I want to go to college more than anything! But I just can't let you go to my house. My dad— Sometimes my dad gets…rough. And Pastor Stevens knows—'' Her voice broke on a sob.

Angela put her arm around the girl's tense shoulders. ''Never mind, Cathy. You don't have to explain. I understand.'' She ignored a sudden twinge of nerves and forced a smile. ''Why don't you go splash some cold water on your eyes while I call the church? It will make them feel better.'' She pointed to the door that led to the entrance hall. ''Go through there and make a right—it's the door on the right side.''

When Cathy had gone, Angela drew a deep breath, turned to the phone and tapped the memory button for the church. Closing her eyes, she forced herself to pray against her own wishes while the phone on the other end of the line rang. ''Please let him be there for Cathy's sake, Lord. Please let him—''

''Hello. Christian Crossroads—''

''Barbara, this is Angela. Sorry to interrupt, but I need to talk to Pastor Stevens right away. Is he there?''

''Yes. Hold on, Angela.''

''Thanks.'' Angela glanced up at the clock. Only six hours until Cathy had to be at Middleton. Subtract four hours of steady driving to get there, and it didn't leave—''

''Hello, Miss Warren. What can I do for you?''

Angela closed her eyes and gripped the edge of the counter as the deep, full voice came over the line. ''Hello, Pastor Stevens. I have a small emergency involving a young lady from the church—Cathy Anders. And I need some help. I'm sorry to bother you, but you're the only one she will let me call. Would it be possible for you to come—?''

''Where are you?''

''At my house.''

''The address?''

''Twenty-seven South Logan.''

''I'll be right there.''

The phone went dead. Angela hung up, pushed aside the jittery qualm the thought of seeing Hosea Stevens outside of church caused, grabbed the piece of paper on which she had written the number for the college registrar's office and punched in the numbers.

''Registrar's office.''

''Hello. I'd like to speak with someone concerning the registration of a student—Cathy Anders.'' Angela smiled, reached into the refrigerator and pulled out a pitcher of lemonade as Cathy walked back into the kitchen.

''I'm sorry, it's too late to consider a new student. Registration closes at four o'clock this afternoon.''

''Yes, I know.'' Angela poured a glassful of the cool liquid, handed it to Cathy, then directed her attention back to the woman on the phone. ''I'm calling because a problem with transportation has cropped up and I want to pay what Cathy owes with my credit card right now to secure her scholarship and classes.''

''I'm sorry. That's against Middleton College policy. The instructions we send upon acceptance of a student clearly state that students must appear in person to register and secure their classes.''

Angela frowned. ''But, surely, you must have some sort of contingency plan for emergencies.''

''I'm sorry. But to allow you to pay over the phone

would not be fair to those students who have made the effort to be here on time.''

''I see. Very well. Thank you for your time.'' Angela refrained from slamming the receiver down, and walked over to put her arm around the teenager who had turned her back to hide her tears.

''Don't cry, Cathy. It's going to be all right. It's just going to be a little more difficult than I thought. But, I promise you this, nothing is impossible with the Lord.''

The front doorbell rang.

Angela's heart leaped into her throat. She gave the girl's shoulders an encouraging squeeze. ''There's the pastor now.'' She hurried to the front door and yanked it open before she gave in to her urge to run and hide.

''Hello, Pastor Stevens. Thank you for coming so quickly.'' Angela stepped out onto the porch and moved aside to make room for Cathy to follow.

Hosea nodded. His gaze swept to the girl's tense face. ''Hello, Cathy, I understand you have a problem.''

The concern and compassion in his voice whisked Angela's mind back to the night in the Crossroads Church when she had been born again. She said a quick prayer that the situation wouldn't cause Hosea Stevens's mind to make that same leap, then, taking a deep breath, she plunged into her request.

''I'm so glad you're here, Pastor, but I can't ask you in because time is of the essence. It's imperative Cathy be at Middleton College before four o'clock this afternoon to save her scholarship and register for classes. It's a four-hour drive to Middleton and time is getting short.''

She took another breath as Hosea checked his watch. "I'm going to drive her to Middleton—that's settled. The problem is…well…Cathy won't let me take her home to get her things.''

She looked up at Hosea with a silent plea in her eyes. "That's why I called you. If you will be so kind as to take Cathy home so she can get her things, and then bring her back here as quickly as possible so we can be on our way, it will help tremendously. I promise to explain everything to you as soon as I can.''

For a long, moment Hosea Stevens simply looked at her, and then, to her immense relief, he nodded and turned to the teenager. "You'll have to give me directions to your house, Cathy. I'm not totally familiar with the streets of Harmony just yet.''

Angela relaxed. For a moment, when he had looked at her, she had thought… She shook her head and straightened as Hosea walked Cathy to his car. If he had remembered her past, so be it. At least Cathy would be out of that house and free from the tyranny of her alcoholic father.

Angela blinked sudden moisture from her eyes and went inside to change out of her dress clothes into something more comfortable for the trip as Hosea drove away.

Thirty-five minutes gone. Angela dragged her gaze from the clock, stuffed bananas, apples, a bag of cookies and a container of mixed nuts into a wicker basket, tossed some paper napkins on top, then added a thermos of lemonade and some cups. What else? A jacket. She would need a jacket when it cooled off later.

She grabbed the basket and her purse, hurried to the hall closet, selected a blue-plaid blazer that looked good with the jeans and soft, ribbed-cotton turtleneck she was wearing, then stood nibbling on her bottom lip as she tried to think of anything else they might need. There would be no time to stop for anything. Her sunglasses! She had left them on the kitchen counter.

Forty-two minutes gone. ''Lord, please help us make it in time!''

Too nervous to stay inside, Angela locked the front door and walked to her car. She placed the basket on the floor in the back, tossed her blazer and purse on the seat, then closed the car door and stared up the road. The relief that swept through her when Hosea Stevens's car came around the corner and rolled to a stop at the curb was so intense she could have cried.

The thought that her emotional involvement in Cathy's problem was way out of line with their casual relationship flitted across her mind as she ran to help transfer the teenager's things to her car.

''Sorry we took so long. I know the timing is tight.'' Hosea lifted one of the smaller pieces of worn, mismatched luggage from his trunk, added a tattered bed pillow and handed them both to Angela.

She darted her gaze to Cathy who was carrying a paper bag full of books across the lawn toward the Saab in the driveway. One look at the girl's tense posture told her what had caused the delay. She glanced back at Hosea. "I'm sorry. I was hoping her father wouldn't be there. I was hoping—" She sighed. "Did he make a drunken scene?"

Hosea stuck a small case under his arm and grabbed up another larger one. "He tried to. We didn't oblige."

Angela's face drew taut. She still remembered the horrible embarrassment she had suffered whenever her parents had made a public display. "Is Cathy all right?"

"No. But she will be. I sent her to wait in the car while I got her things." Hosea freed a hand and closed the trunk lid. It slammed down.

Angela jumped.

"Sorry. I didn't mean to do that." Hosea took a long breath.

I sent her to wait in the car. Those simple words said so much. She stole a quick glance at him. A man like Hosea would have helped her when her parents... She shook her head sharply to drive away the thought. What was done, was done. It did no good to dwell on it. She cleared the lump from her throat.

"Thank you, Pastor. Thank you for helping Cathy." She didn't look at him. The memories of her past were so strong she was afraid of what he might read in her eyes—and what he might remember because of it. Hugging the tattered pillow against her chest, she started for her car.

"No thanks are needed, Miss Warren, it's what I do." He fell into step beside her. "I take care of God's children, remember?"

Remember? Angela nodded and looked down at the ground. *Remember?*

"I'll take those, Miss Warren."

Angela jolted to a stop and looked up.

Cathy gave her a nervous smile. "You need to open the trunk."

"Oh, of course. Thanks." Grateful for the excuse to leave Hosea Stevens's side, Angela hurried to the car, pushed the button to unlock the trunk, then grabbed a map from the glove compartment and pretended to study it.

"Well, I think that's everything." Hosea tucked in the pillow, closed the trunk and smiled at Cathy. "I'll be expecting to hear a good report on your college experience when you come home over the holiday break."

Cathy nodded and moved forward to pull open the passenger door. "Thank you for your help with…with everything, Pastor Stevens. I'm sorry for—"

Hosea lifted a hand to halt her words. "You've nothing to be sorry for, Cathy, I was pleased to help. Now, you'd better climb in." He smiled at her and turned toward the driver's side of the car.

Angela hastily tossed the map on the dash, slid into her seat and pulled the door shut.

Hosea braced his hands on the window ledge and leaned down to look at her. "I'll be praying you have a safe and successful trip, Miss Warren."

"Thank you." She glanced up at him through her open window. "Thank you for everything." She fastened her seat belt, glanced at her watch and reached for the key. Right now she wanted to be away from Hosea Stevens as much as she wanted to get Cathy to the college on time.

She twisted the key. The starter engaged, the motor turned over and…nothing.

Angela stared in disbelief at the key, then twisted it again. Nothing. *Lord, please!* She tried again, with the same result.

"What's wrong?"

Angela jerked her head toward Cathy at the tense, softly spoken words.

"I don't know. My car's never done this before." She reached over and laid a comforting hand on Cathy's arm as the girl bit down on her lip and turned her head away. "It's not a problem, Cathy. I'll just go call the rental company and we'll be on our way." She grabbed her purse and dug for her house key.

Is this your intervention, Lord? Hosea's pulse kicked up a notch at the thought.

He reached down and opened Angela's door. "There's not enough time for that, Miss Warren." He gave her a warm smile that included Cathy as well. "We'll take my car."

Angela's eyes widened. He thought she was about to refuse, then she bit down on her lip and reached down to push the button that opened the trunk.

"You're right. There isn't time to arrange for a rental car. Thank you, Pastor." She yanked the key from the ignition, grabbed the things from the back seat, and headed for his car.

Chapter Five

The lines seemed endless to Angela, but at last the cashier was paid, Cathy's scholarship and classes secured, her college ID and meal ticket purchased, her books bought and her dorm room claimed. For dinner, Hosea Stevens took them to a wonderful old mill that had been converted into a restaurant, presently overflowing with college students and parents. The evening was capped off by a hasty trip to local stores for needed supplies. Now, it was time to leave. Angela gave Cathy a final, encouraging hug, then walked across the parking lot beside Hosea.

She was exhausted. The painful memories brought so forcibly to the fore throughout the day, combined with the strain of sifting every nuance from every word Hosea Stevens spoke, had been wearying in the extreme. She felt like one of those overcooked strands in a can of spaghetti—and she still had to endure the long ride home alone with him.

That thought made Angela's stomach roil. She

should have skipped dinner. She stopped beside the car.

"Well, that was a job well done, Miss Warren." Hosea unlocked the car and held her door while she took her seat. "I'm sure Cathy will do well in her studies—she's highly motivated if winning a scholastic scholarship in spite of her troubling situation is any indication." He slid into the driver's seat and snapped his seat belt in place. "I think her greatest growth will probably be personal and social. It can't be easy to make and keep friends when you live in such a difficult home environment. You must feel immense satisfaction for having made all this possible for her."

What she felt was nervous! Angela edged as far toward her door as her seat restraint would allow. "She told you?"

"That you paid her share of everything? Yes." Hosea twisted his key in the ignition and the motor roared to life. "That was very generous of you."

Angela's cheeks heated at the warm approval in his voice. "It wasn't that much. Not when you compare it to what it would have been if she hadn't had the scholarships and work program."

Heavens, she was babbling like an idiot! She folded the strap of her purse and tucked it into the elasticized pocket on the side. "Anyway, it was the Lord who provided for Cathy. I had received an unexpected bonus today."

Hosea put the car in reverse, then twisted around and laid his arm on the back of the seat to look out the rear window. "I didn't know about the bonus, of course, but I don't doubt for a moment the provision was from the Lord.''

He backed neatly from the parking space, put the car in gear and glanced her way as they exited the parking lot. "What I meant was, you chose to give of His provision to Cathy. You could have kept it all for yourself. Including the bonus.''

Angela shook her head. "Not after I saw Cathy crying in the park and heard her story. No one could have.''

"Unfortunately, there are a lot of people who would still have kept the money for themselves." Hosea checked his mirror, then pulled over to join the stream of traffic headed for the interstate. "That's why God chose you to help Cathy...He knows your heart.''

Now what did he mean by that? The man was a master of ambiguity! Did he mean God used her to bless Cathy because He knew she was unselfish—or because He knew she would relate to Cathy's situation because of her past?

Angela sighed, laid her hands on top of her purse in her lap, and thrust the troubling thoughts away. She was only making herself more nervous. And maybe— just maybe—she was reading things into what he said because of her guilt.

She stole a quick, guarded look at Hosea as he maneuvered the car into the line of vehicles entering the interstate highway. It had proved a real blessing for Cathy to have him with them today. His quiet air of authority had facilitated matters more than once—and his kindness to the upset teenager had been like balm to her tense nerves. He had been patient, gentle, understanding…and funny.

Angela's lips twitched at the memory of his running commentary on the other diners and servers at the restaurant. It had been hilarious, but never cruel or mean-spirited. And she knew he had done it to put Cathy at ease. It was obvious the teenager was not used to dining in fine restaurants. All in all, Hosea Stevens seemed a thoroughly nice man. But nice could be an illusion—she should know.

Angela shivered. What on earth was she doing alone in a car with Hosea Stevens? He might be a pastor, but he was still a man, and it was a four-hour trip home.

The car accelerated. Angela leaned her head back and closed her eyes. Maybe if she pretended to be asleep he would leave her alone. Maybe. A rustle of movement made her pop her eyes open again.

Hosea glanced at her and smiled. ''I'm sorry, I didn't mean to disturb you. You've had a pretty hectic day and I thought maybe some music would be in order. I know it helps me to unwind.'' He nodded toward the center console. ''The CDs are in there. But, it's no problem if you'd rather not.''

Angela's cheeks burned. Had he guessed what she had thought? ''Music would be nice.'' And it might keep you from talking, or remembering about me, she thought. She took a deep breath.

Hosea shot her another quick look. ''Choose whatever you like. I've a little of everything. Classical, country, R and B, and, of course, Christian praise and—''

Angela held up her hand. "You choose."

"All right." Hosea flipped open the console, pulled out a CD and popped it into the player. "This is one of my 'unwinding' favorites." The rich sound of a saxophone duet filled the car. He lowered the volume and turned his attention back to his driving.

"I thought Cathy's roommate seemed nice. What did you think of her?"

More small talk? *So much for the music distracting him.* Angela turned her head to look at him. "I thought she was very friendly and outgoing."

Hosea nodded. "I think she'll probably be a big help to Cathy as she adjusts to college life—especially in the social area. She struck me as the type who always knows where she is and what she's about. But I think Cathy will be an even bigger help to her—spiritually speaking that is."

Angela stared at him. "You gleaned all that from the few minutes we spoke with her?"

He gave her a lopsided grin. "Pastor's antenna."

"Really? And you look so normal."

Hosea laughed at the dry comment. "They're not working right now."

Good thing! The bitter thought erased Angela's smile. She turned her head to look out the window.

"You said you saw Cathy crying in the park. That's a beautiful drive along the river. Do you go that way often?"

"No." Angela shook her head. "It's quite a bit out of my way. I just had a sudden impulse to go that way this morning." She leaned back against the seat and brushed a wisp of hair from her cheek. "I guess it's fortunate I did."

"Yes, indeed."

"Still, if it hadn't been for a car full of children and picnic supplies I would have missed Cathy."

"Oh?" He shot her a questioning look.

Angela related the story to him.

"Hmm. An unexpected bonus, a sudden impulse to change routes, an urge to walk along the river, and a bird that directed your attention to Cathy. Sounds as if God has been in this situation from the beginning."

Angela gaped at him. "It does, doesn't it?"

He stole a quick, sidelong look at her. "You sound surprised."

"I *am* surprised."

"Why? God does this sort of thing all the time. He takes care of his children."

"Yes, I know. But you're saying He used *me*."

He stole another look at her. "Why shouldn't He? You're His child."

"Yes, but—" Angela stiffened and clamped her mouth shut. Her pulse pounded. She had almost blurted out the truth! She had almost said God wouldn't use an ex-prostitute.

"But what?" Hosea flipped on his blinker and passed a red SUV that blocked his forward view.

"Nothing. It was nothing important." Angela blanked her mind the way she had during the bad times in her past. It was a trick she'd learned to protect her spirit and ease the ache in her heart. She closed her eyes and concentrated on the music.

Hosea glanced at Angela's tense, strained profile

and his hands tightened on the steering wheel. *Lord, she's hurting! How do I help her?*

There was no answer. He let out a long, deep sigh and concentrated on his driving. He'd heard that weighted silence before.

"Miss Warren?"

Angela started and opened her eyes. The moon and stars shining through the sun roof illuminated Hosea Stevens's face. She gasped and bolted upright.

"You're home."

She glanced out the side window. They were parked at the curb in front of her house. A rush of blood heated her cheeks at the thought of her mistrust of him. Not to mention the fact that she had fallen asleep. "Pastor Stevens, I'm so sorry."

"No need to apologize, Miss Warren. You've had an eventful, not to say, tiring, day. Being a Good Samaritan can be emotionally exhausting work—especially if you're not used to it." He smiled, got out, and came around the car to open her door. "Of course, I'm assuming you don't rescue young women in distress every day. At least not in such an intense, time-pressured fashion."

"You assume correctly. Still—"

He quirked an eyebrow and chuckled. "I'm teasing you, Miss Warren."

Angela swallowed the rest of the apology. She gave him a polite smile instead. "Thank you for your help, Pastor. If you hadn't offered your car, I'm afraid this day would have ended very differently."

She slid her gaze to the silver Saab in her driveway

and shook her head. "I just can't imagine what happened to my car. It's never done that before. It's very reliable"

"Why don't you give me your keys. I'll see if it will start before I leave."

"Oh, no. I couldn't ask—"

"You didn't." Hosea smiled and held out his hand.

Reluctantly, Angela dug into her purse, gave him her keys and followed him to her car. He got in and turned the key in the ignition. The engine purred to life. Her mouth gaped open.

Hosea turned off the car, started it again, then shut it off and climbed out. "It seems to be working fine now." He handed her the key.

Angela looked at it as if she'd never seen it before. "I don't understand." She looked from her car to Hosea's smiling face. "Why didn't it start this afternoon?"

"I can't say, Miss Warren." He nodded toward the basket she held. "Would you like me to carry that to the door for you?"

"What? Oh. No. I'm fine. Thank you." She started for her front door. Was it her imagination, or did he look pleased?

"I'll say good night, now, Miss Warren. Have a pleasant night's rest."

Angela turned. He had stopped at the bottom of the porch steps. "Thank you. And you rest well, too, Pastor Stevens."

"Oh, I certainly will, Miss Warren." He smiled, gave her a small, jaunty salute and walked to his car whistling a tune she vaguely recognized.

She unlocked her door and went inside.

It was as she was climbing the stairs to her bedroom the song Hosea had whistled came back into Angela's mind. She hummed the melody softly as she prepared for bed, but try as she might, she couldn't think of the words. All she could remember was it said something about God working in mysterious ways.

Chapter Six

"**W**ell, I finally made it—Africa has arrived!" Leigh set the large carton she was carrying down on the floor beside the one with Colombia scrawled across it in bright-red ink and glanced over at Angela. "Sorry, I'm late. Why don't you let me finish ironing those things while you start arranging the table decorations? I can't wait to see how they look."

Angela whipped the dark-blue linen cloth off the ironing board, pulled the plug on the iron and turned to give her friend a mock scowl. "Great timing, Leigh. This is the last one."

Leigh glanced at the long tables that filled the room—they were all covered with snowy white cloth. "Well, I guess I *did* time that perfectly." She grinned at Angela, picked up the box marked Center Serving Table and carried it over to set on the floor at her feet. "Here you are, my friend. Do you want the other tables set up in any particular order?"

Angela lifted a large globe out of the box and placed

it in the center of the sea of dark-blue linen she had just spread on the table. "Not really. Alphabetical is always good."

She pulled various candles, exotic silk flowers and fake fruits and vegetables out of the box and began arranging them in an artful display that climbed the base of the globe and spilled across the table on either side of it.

"Okay. Alphabetical it is. I'll get to it as soon as I take care of *that* little problem." Leigh gestured toward the large banner they had made, grinned, then headed across the room toward her fiancé.

"Phil, that banner is creased in the center. Look at that poor elephant's trunk. He'll need remedial surgery if you don't straighten it out."

Angela laughed.

Philip Johnson glanced back at the black-felt elephant that marched in single file with other animal silhouettes across the top of the missionary banner. Its trunk was definitely askew. He gave a low growl, tucked his package of tacks in his shirt pocket and climbed down to move the ladder he was standing on back under the elephant.

"You'll have to redo all the tacks back as far as the lion to straighten it out."

Phil glanced at Leigh who was standing squinting up at the banner, gave a loud, fake sigh, and moved the ladder to stand under the lion. "Are you going to be this bossy after we're married?"

Leigh nodded. "When it comes to my fields of expertise—you betcha!"

''Woe is me!'' Phil rolled his eyes and started up the ladder.

Leigh laughed. ''There's still time to change your mind.''

Phil stopped climbing and looked down at his bride-to-be. ''Never, Leigh. Never in a million years.''

Angela's hands stilled. It hit her, with sudden, unexpected force, that she would never have that. She would never know how it felt to have a man look at her with love in his eyes, or speak to her with love in his voice. No decent man would ever love a woman with a past like hers. And love could not be based on deceit.

Oh, what did it matter? She didn't want to be involved with anyone. How could she ever trust a man? A sense of loss swept through her. She ignored it, reached for the candles and began inserting them in the assorted brass holders.

''Angela, I love this!'' Leigh placed a small grass hut in the middle of the Africa table and stepped back to look at it. ''When did you make it?''

''Last night.''

''Really? You must have been up late. It was after eleven when we finished cutting out the silhouettes.''

Leigh turned back to the box and began setting out the miniature replicas of African animals. ''Hey! I just had a thought.'' She added a lion to the collection. ''When we're through here, let's go get a pizza. I'm starved.''

''You're always starved.'' Phil gave a sad shake of his head. ''I can see our grocery bills now.''

Leigh stuck her tongue out at him.

He laughed, blew her a kiss, and looked across the room. "How about it, Angela? Could you tuck away some pizza later?"

Angela grinned at him and opened a bag of potpourri to sprinkle among the fruits and flowers she'd arranged around the globe. The heady scent of exotic flowers wafted upward. "If you can make Leigh behave, I might agree to go for pizza."

"Pizza? Did I hear someone mention pizza?"

Both women jumped and spun around.

Hosea Stevens stepped out of the doorway into the room. "Sorry, ladies, I didn't mean to startle you. I was working in my office and heard voices, so I thought I'd come investigate."

"Well you just knocked five years off my life expectancy, Pastor!" Leigh placed her hand over her heart and pretended to swoon. "As for pizza, don't expect me to invite you to join us after that scare. You'll just have to try to wrangle an invitation out of Angela."

Hosea grinned at her. "Is that a challenge, Dr. Roberts?"

Leigh ignored the frantic head shake Angela gave her behind Hosea's back and nodded. "It is."

"I see. Well, in that case...I accept." Hosea turned and walked over to Angela. "How about it, Miss Warren? Are you more gracious and forgiving than your friend here?" He jerked his head backward to indicate the laughing Leigh. "Or will I have to go to my office and contemplate the error of my ways in lonely starvation?"

"Oh, foul play!"

Hosea laughed at Leigh's pained cry. "Well, Miss Warren?"

How could she refuse? Angela put down the plastic melon she held in her hand before she squeezed it out of shape—or beaned Leigh with it. "That won't be necessary, Pastor Stevens." She pretended not to see Leigh who was grinning and waggling her eyebrows at her. "I'm much more gracious than Leigh. Ask anyone who knows us, they'll tell you that's true."

"Oh!" Leigh grabbed the knife she had used to slit open the carton and held it out in front of her. "Why don't you just stick this in my heart, *friend*?"

Angela glanced down at the knife, then looked up at Leigh and laughed. "Don't tempt me. A knife wielded by my unskilled hand would be terribly messy."

Leigh's mouth gaped open.

Phil burst into laughter and backed down the ladder to put his arm around his bride-to-be. "Now this is something you don't see too often, Pastor—Leigh speechless." He dropped a kiss on her hair. "He bested you, sweetheart."

"Traitor!" Leigh pretended to glare at him. "I may have been bested by the pastor, but I know how to fix your wagon." She gave him a diabolical grin. "I'm going to order extra toppings."

"No!" Phil clasped his hands in abject supplication. "Please, I beg of you, Leigh, anything but that."

It was all so foolish—and so fun. Angela turned away and busied herself placing the candles among the flowers so the others wouldn't notice the sudden, hard-to-explain tears in her eyes.

* * *

"No, no. I disagree with the ref's call. He was inside the line when he made that catch!"

Hosea grinned at Phil and shook his head. "Sorry, friend, he may be your favorite receiver, but his right foot was over the line."

"Leigh?"

"Don't look to me for succor, you traitor." Leigh grinned at Phil and reached for another piece of pizza. "The man was outside."

Phil groaned and looked across the table. "Angela?"

She shook her head, "Sorry, Phil. I didn't see the game."

"Oh, I forgot. You were at Pine Glen."

Hosea looked her way. "You have a relative at the nursing home, Miss Warren?"

The polite address sounded out of place in the midst of the informal fun. Angela pushed her plate away and looked across the table. "No. I just borrow them. I have no living relatives. And please, call me Angela, Pastor. Miss Warren is much too formal for this crew."

"Hey!"

Hosea laughed at Leigh's response. "I couldn't agree more…Angela."

The smile he gave her stole her breath away. Or maybe it was the sudden dig of Leigh's elbow in her ribs. She looked down at her plate.

Beep…beep…beep…

"Oh, no! Not now. This thing always goes off when I'm eating." Leigh grabbed for the pager in her purse, read the message and sighed. "Let's go, Phil, Mrs.

Paltro's time has arrived." She grabbed a napkin and began to wrap a piece of pizza in it while Phil pulled out his wallet.

"It's a good thing you drove your car, Pastor— otherwise you and Angela might be enjoying the dubious comfort of the third floor waiting room for the next few hours." Leigh rose to her feet, turned so only Angela could see, gave her a surreptitious thumbs-up and headed for the door.

Angela wanted to choke her—or beg her to take her with her. What she didn't want was to be left alone with Hosea Stevens. She stared down at the money Phil had tossed onto the red-checked tablecloth and tried desperately to think of a reasonable excuse to refuse the ride home he was sure to offer. Her mind refused to cooperate. It locked on the thought of the intimate confines of his car and refused to budge.

"They're quite a pair."

"What? Oh. Yes. They are." Angela smoothed a crease from her napkin, then crumpled it and tossed it onto the table beside her plate. "Leigh is wonderful. She's warm and kind and enthusiastic. And fun. She's lots of fun. And Phil is perfect for her. He has the same wonderful qualities. God did good work when He matched those two."

Angela lifted her gaze from her plate and searched the restaurant for a friend. Surely there was someone else here with whom she could ride home.

"That's not very surprising, considering God's wisdom is perfect."

Angela looked over at Hosea and curved her lips in a polite smile. "That's true. It is."

"What about you, Angela?" Hosea reached for his soda and took a swallow. "Has God done a good work in you?"

Angela's heart stopped—then beat furiously. She clasped her hands in her lap and straightened her shoulders. If he was going to bring up her past he would have to spell it out, she wasn't going to help him. "I'm sorry, I don't know what you mean."

"Has God matched *you* up with a perfect some-one?"

The starch went out of Angela's spine. She looked down so he wouldn't see the relief in her eyes and shook her head. "Oh, I see. No. No one—perfect or otherwise." The small joke came out sounding flat.

Hosea nodded and set his glass down. "Perhaps the time has not been right. But when it is, God will reveal to you the one He has chosen as your mate. After all, He's the one that truly knows your heart."

He pulled some bills from his wallet, tossed them down on top of the money Phil had left, and looked across the table. "Are you ready?"

"Yes." Angela was almost giddy with relief. He would never have made such a statement if he had re-membered her past. He would know, as surely as she did, God would never choose her as a mate for any man. At least not any decent man. She was soiled goods.

The thought turned her stomach sour. She took a sip of water, then reached for her purse as Hosea rose to his feet.

The music swelled, then softened as the strings picked up the melody. Ordinarily, Angela would have enjoyed the wonderful sound; she liked classical music. Tonight, however, she was too aware of the man beside her to relax.

"Which way now? I'm not familiar with this area yet."

Angela looked out at the familiar intersection. "Turn left onto Green Street, then left again onto Logan."

Hosea nodded, flicked on his blinker, turned the corner, then turned again. Before Angela could think what to do when they reached her house the car stopped. She dug into her purse for her keys and turned to thank Hosea for the ride home but she wasn't quick enough—he was already climbing from his seat. He slammed his door shut and started around the car.

Lord, please, let him say good-night right here at the car and leave. Please!

The door latch clicked. Angela pasted a smile onto her face and slid from the seat as Hosea pulled the door open. The sweet, dusky scent of the last of her neighbor's prize roses rushed toward her on the warm autumn air. It didn't help her stomach. She swallowed hard and held out her hand. "Thank you for the ride, Pastor. I—" She stopped as he shook his head.

"My mom would be very disappointed in me if I left before seeing you to your door. Good manners were stressed in our house."

He smiled, gave an appreciative sniff of the scented air, then tipped his head back to look up at the star-filled sky. "What a beautiful night. You don't see stars like this in the city."

Angela tensed. Was his reference to the city a subtle hint? "No, I guess not. I suppose smog closes them out." She started up the brick sidewalk to her porch.

Hosea strolled along beside her. "I meant to tell you earlier how great the fellowship hall looks. The decorations are certainly unique." He took the keys from her hand. "You and Leigh really are creative."

"Thank you. I'm glad you're pleased." Angela reached out and touched one of the keys. "It's that one."

Hosea nodded, unlocked the door and gave her back the keys. "There's something I've been meaning to ask you—"

The keys fell from Angela's suddenly nerveless fingers. They hit the porch floor with a dull clank.

Hosea bent to pick them up. "I was about to ask if you are going to bring apple pie to the Missionary Conference dinner Saturday night." He gave her a sheepish grin. "I've been thinking a lot about that cinnamon syrup you make."

Angela stared at him. She had been scared to death, and all he had wanted to ask about was pie! Hysterical laughter bubbled up and threatened to burst from her throat. The corners of her lips twitched. She pressed her fingernails into her palms to control the laughter.

"Pretty brazen, huh?" Hosea ran a hand through his hair. "I apologize. I'm not usually so bold. But you bake the best apple pie I've ever been privileged to eat."

Angela dipped her head. "Thanks. I'll be happy to bake apple pies for the dinner."

"Great! I'll look forward to that. Well, until Saturday night then.'' He turned to leave, paused on the first step, and looked back at her. ''Good night, Angela Warren.''

The look in his eyes was as soft and warm as the night air. Angela's knees went weak. She grabbed behind her for the solid support of the doorknob. ''Good night, Pastor Stevens.''

It was relief. That's what she told herself. It was relief that he hadn't confronted her with her past. That's why she had suddenly gone breathless, and wobbly in the knees. It was the relief. Angela told herself that until she believed it. Anything else was too scary to contemplate.

It was getting serious. Hosea frowned and jabbed the power button on the remote to shut off the TV. He couldn't concentrate on the news. All he could think about was Angela. She was such a warm, giving, talented, beautiful woman. And the way her hair fell in those little wisps against her temples drove him crazy! And her eyes...

Hosea surged to his feet. She had such incredible, expressive eyes! But when she was off guard you could see the pain in their depths. Was he right? Had her past never been dealt with? ''Lord, I need Your wisdom. Please help me to help Angela.''

Chapter Seven

"**W**ell that was an unqualified success!" Leigh carried two glasses of iced tea to a table, plopped down in a folding chair, propped her feet up on an another and wiggled her toes. "My feet tell me so."

Angela laughed. "Really? Maybe that emergency C-section you had to perform just before the dinner has something to do with your aching feet."

"Hmm, maybe. But the dinner was fabulous. And everyone loved your decorations."

"Our." Angela put the last decoration in a box and closed the top.

Leigh snorted at the correction. "We both know who does the decorating and who does the running and fetching. You're the talent. I'm the drone…or mechanic…or something like that. I'm too tired to think straight." She hid a yawn behind her hand.

Angela added the box to the stack by the door, then walked to the table and slid onto a chair. "Why don't you go on home, Leigh? Everything is packed up. I can carry the boxes to my car.''

Leigh shook her head. ''I'm not going anywhere. I've been waiting all night for this moment. Now out with it. Tell me!''

''Tell you what?'' Angela squeezed lemon on top of the ice cubes floating in her tea and stirred.

Leigh leaned forward. ''What happened Thursday night?''

Angela took a swallow of her tea. ''Nothing happened.''

''Nothing?''

''Nothing. What did you expect? And while we're on the subject—thanks for putting me in that position.'' Angela gave Leigh a level look over the top of the frosty glass. ''You know how I feel about dating.''

Leigh waved away her protest. ''It wasn't a date, it just happened. But I thought…''

''You thought what?''

Leigh waggled her eyebrows. ''You know… *whoosh!*''

''Oh, Leigh, for goodness'—''

''Uh-uh-uh!'' Leigh wagged her finger in the air between them. ''Don't protest too much, Angela. It makes me suspicious. I was at that table with you two Thursday evening.'' She lifted her hands and fluttered her fingers. ''Spark, spark, crackle, crackle! The electricity in the air was enough to make my hair stand on end.''

''Oh, don't be silly! The man's a pastor.'' Angela plunked her glass back down on the table a little too sharply—tea sloshed over the brim.

Leigh grinned and handed her a paper napkin. "He's also a man. A nice…handsome… *single*…man."

"And *I* am a single woman." Angela wiped up the spilled tea, then wadded the napkin into a ball. "And I intend to stay that way."

"Uh-huh."

"Oh…you're impossible!" Angela jumped to her feet, stepped over to the bar that separated the fellowship hall from the adjoining kitchen and threw the napkin in the trash basket.

Leigh chuckled. "There was something happening between you two all right. I wasn't sure before—but I am now. I've never seen you so agitated."

Angela made an inarticulate sound and grabbed a leftover bag of ginger snaps off the counter.

"What are you doing?"

"I'm getting a cookie!" Angela ripped the bag open and reached inside.

Leigh's lips twitched. "I thought you said you were stuffed."

"I *am* stuffed." Angela shot her a look. "I just want to *bite* something!"

Leigh let out a wild whoop, and collapsed against the table with laughter.

Angela glared at her, jammed the cookie back into the bag, then marched over and picked up one of the boxes. She could hear Leigh laughing all the way to her car.

Why was this happening? Had God brought Pastor Hosea Stevens back into her life to make her move to another town? What did He want from her? Oh, the whole situation was just a big, confusing mess!

Angela rolled out of bed, threw an oversize T-shirt on over her pajamas, and stomped barefoot down to the kitchen.

Why did Leigh have to say anything about Thursday night? How could she deny to herself the attraction she felt for Hosea Stevens if it was obvious to others? And what was worse—now she couldn't pretend that look she had seen in his eyes was a figment of her imagination. But surely the strange new sensations she was experiencing were caused by her fear of discovery and the resulting emotional turmoil that brought about. It certainly wasn't love—or God revealing his choice of a mate for her. That idea was ridiculous. Laughable! She was the last person God would want as a wife for one of his servants.

Those thoughts hurt. Angela drew a deep breath, expelled it in a long, slow sigh and padded out onto the back porch. She was so tired of living with the pain of her past.

The cool night air caressed her skin. The scent of her neighbor's roses took her back to Thursday night—to the very moment she wanted to forget. The moment when Hosea Stevens had turned to say good-night and the warmth in his voice and eyes had begun to melt the wall of ice she had erected around her heart when she was twelve.

Angela shuddered and closed her eyes as the memories came crashing back. She would never understand how a mother could act as her mother had, but nothing could change the past. Her mother and stepfather were dead. Killed by the drug they craved so badly they had forced her into prostitution to pay for it.

The shuddering increased. Angela wrapped her arms around herself but it didn't help. The cold was inside—deep inside. Her teeth chattered. *Lord, please! Please stop the memories!*

The plea was too late. The images were already swirling through her mind. The terror of being locked in a bedroom with strange men had already gripped her.

Angela whirled and ran to the living room sofa, burying her face in a pillow to muffle the sound of her sobs. Even though she lived alone, the habit was a strong one. She had never let anyone hear her cry.

Angela stared at her reflection in the bathroom mirror. The cold cloth hadn't helped; her eyes were still puffy. She heaved a sigh, brushed a hint of color across her cheeks, put moisturizing gloss on her lips, then went into the bedroom to dress. If she timed it right, she could arrive at church just as Hosea started preaching.

The sunlight pouring in through the double windows of her bedroom dormer drew her attention. A squirrel raced up the trunk of her oak tree and scurried out to the end of a branch to gather acorns. Chickadees and nuthatches darted about, breakfasting on the sunflower seeds in the bird feeder she had made from a chicken crate. She smiled at their antics and dropped her gaze to Mac, the neighbor's Scottie dog, who was curled up on the padded seat of her lawn swing fast asleep. Oh, dear, she'd have to vacuum it again.

Tears welled into Angela's eyes. She loved her house. It was the only home she had ever had, but was God trying to make her leave it as punishment for her past?

Angela fought the thought with everything that was in her. *A loving God wouldn't do that.* She stood bathed in the sunlight streaming in through the windows and told herself that over, and over, and over again. But the guilt from her past defeated her. She stepped back out of the golden rays of light, wiped the tears from her eyes, and went to her closet.

The gray silk suit best fit her mood. Angela frowned, pushed the suit aside, and put on a bronze-colored dress in a soft fabric that lightly skimmed over her body before it flared into a long skirt that ended a few inches above her ankles. She stepped into the matching shoes, went to the dresser, fastened a thin gold chain about her neck, put her gold watch on her wrist and inserted her favorite small, gold, twisted-knot earrings.

She was ready.

She glanced at her alarm clock. Perfect! She had just enough time to drive to church. She picked up her Bible and went downstairs.

That had worked out nicely. But how long would her ploy of late arrival, early exit from church work? Angela pushed the thought away, turned into the Pine Glen Nursing Home parking lot and climbed from her car. She would worry about avoiding Hosea Stevens next Sunday; for now, she would just enjoy her time with Sophie and the others.

The sun warmed Angela's face, and a gentle breeze riffled her short hair and stirred the long skirt of her dress as she crossed the parking lot. A bird, perched on the entrance canopy, sang out its content with the beautiful day. The door buzzer sounded, and she pulled open the door and stepped inside as the bird flew away.

"Hello there, princess! I was watching for you."

Angela smiled at the elderly gentleman limping toward her. "Hello, Mr. Scott. Thanks for buzzing me in. How are you feeling today?"

"I'm in fine fettle. How about we get Sophie to play us a tune and you dance with me?"

Angela laughed at his standard greeting and shook her head. "Now, Mr. Scott, I've told you…I don't know how to do those fancy ballroom dances. I'd trip you up, and then where would you be?"

"Probably in the hospital." John Scott laughed heartily at his own joke and started down the hall. "Guess I'll go play cards then. But if you change your mind…look me up." He gave her a wink over his shoulder, then chuckled his way down the hall.

Angela turned and headed for Sophie's room. She was anxious to give her "adopted" grandmother the small, lavender sachet she'd bought for her to tuck in her pillow. Sophie had told her that her mother always kept lavender sachets in with her linens and she missed the smell. Angela sighed and rapped lightly on the elderly woman's door. Sophie was having trouble sleeping lately. Maybe the smell of the lavender would help.

Chapter Eight

"**I**'m telling you it's impossible, Angela! For weeks I've been searching for a wedding gown, and I can't find any that I like. Today was no different. Every gown I tried on made me look like a ruffled giraffe…or a beaded elephant, or…or a lace-draped horse!"

Leigh threw herself into the moss green, slubbed-linen chair that sat beside the fireplace in Angela's living room, plopped her long legs across the matching ottoman and glared at her feet.

"You're exaggerating."

"All right, forget the elephant. I'm not fat—I'm just tall. I'm like a…a tree!" Leigh directed her glare at Angela. "Have you ever seen a tree in a wedding gown?"

"Not lately."

Leigh gave a weak smile at the dry comment, leaned her head back and closed her eyes. "Why don't people just get married in jeans and a T-shirt? I can handle that.''

Angela couldn't help but smile at the thought. She set the tray of iced raspberry lemonade she was carrying on the painted trunk she used for a coffee table, sat on the sofa and forced herself to ignore the irony in what she was about to say. ''Why don't I go on the hunt with you tomorrow, Leigh? Time's getting short and—''

Leigh's eyes popped open and she came upright in the chair. ''You'd do that? With your good taste I'm sure to— Wait a minute! What about that research presentation you're working up for Tyler Electronics? Didn't you say you couldn't shop with me because it's due next Tuesday?''

Angela shrugged and poured a glass of the cold liquid. ''It's come along faster than I expected.'' She handed the glass to Leigh and poured another for herself. ''I'll just add the finishing touches to it tonight.''

Leigh's eyes misted. ''You're the best, Angela.'' She lifted her glass into the air. ''To you, compadre. No one ever had a better friend.''

The warmth of Leigh's smile dissolved the cold that had settled around Angela's heart at thought of being around all those symbolically virginal-white gowns. She'd go though a great deal more discomfort than she would suffer tomorrow to make her friend happy. She smiled and lifted her glass toward Leigh. ''Thank you, friend. And—likewise.'' It was the best she could do.

Quickly, she raised the glass to her lips and swallowed, praying the lemonade would slide smoothly past the sudden lump in her throat.

"I think this one."

Leigh leaned forward and looked at the picture of the gown Angela had selected. It was a slim, ivory satin sheath whose only adornments were the pearls on the high neckband and the rich folds of satin that flowed in an inverted vee in the back to form a long, sweeping train.

"What do you think, Leigh?"

"Well…it's—it's awfully plain, Angela. And I'm so plain myself, I don't know."

"You are *not* plain, Leigh." Angela tapped the picture. "And neither is this dress. It's elegant. Will you try it on?"

Leigh shrugged her shoulders. "Sure. It can't make me look any worse than the others did."

"And the size?" The woman helping them turned a knowing glance on Leigh. "Six?"

Leigh glanced at the way the gown slid over the model's figure in the picture and frowned. "Better make it an eight."

"Very well. If you will follow me."

Leigh started after the woman, then turned to Angela and rolled her eyes. "I'll do it. But I'd rather do sixteen hours of nonstop surgery!"

"I still can't believe it. All these weeks I've spent searching, and you find the perfect dress just like that." Leigh snapped her fingers, took a swallow of water, and shook her head.

"I actually felt beautiful. That dress is fantastic! And it's so plain. I don't know how you knew it would look like that." She scooped a bite of cashew-chicken salad onto her fork and looked across the table at Angela. "I wish I had your taste."

Angela forced a smile and pushed her food aside. She shouldn't have ordered. All this bride talk had stolen her appetite. "It wasn't quite that quick, Leigh. We've been shopping all day. And as for taste—you just got caught up in the ruffle-and-lace bride thing. There's nothing wrong with your taste in clothes."

"Right." Leigh grinned, and forked up another bite of salad. "I can choose jeans, shirts and scrubs with the best of them."

Angela laughed and reached for her drink.

Beep…beep…beep…

"Oh, no. Not again! It seems this thing always goes off when I'm eating."

Angela grinned as Leigh shoved another bite of salad in her mouth and grabbed for her pager. "Maybe that's because you're always eating."

"That could be the reason." Leigh grinned and read the message. "Hmm. Looks like we'll have to forget about picking up those things you wanted at the grocery store, Angela—my time off has come to an abrupt end."

She dug into her purse. "I'll have to take you straight home and then head for the hospital. If I can find my keys that is." She scowled, and dug deeper in her purse.

"Home's too far out of your way from here, Leigh. You just head for the hospital."

"No, no. I don't want to leave— Aha!—" Leigh jangled the errant keys in the air in triumph "—you stranded."

"Don't be silly. I'll call a cab."

"Are you sure?"

"Absolutely."

"Thanks, Angela. I really do have to go. But dinner is on me. And so's the cab. That's the least I can do." Leigh tossed some bills onto the table and slid out of the booth. "Thanks, again for today. You saved my life, not to mention my sanity. Truly."

She leaned down and gave Angela a quick hug. "I owe you big!"

The beeps sounded again as Leigh straightened. She sighed. "It's gonna be one of those nights, I can feel it coming." She reached into her purse for the pager. "I can't imagine why this all seemed so glamorous to me in med school."

Angela smiled. "You're only bitter over the loss of dessert. You love every moment of your work and you know it."

Leigh grinned. "You're right…I do. There's something about helping to bring a new life into this world that just—" her face tightened as she scanned the message "—just demands my presence."

She dropped the pager back into her purse, and wiggled her fingers in goodbye. "Sorry about the inconvenience, Angela. I'll try to call you later."

Angela watched Leigh hurry off, then put her drink down on the table, picked up her purse and slid out of the booth. She didn't want the meal—and she didn't want to think about babies. That was another hole in her life that would never be filled. There were a lot of them. Brides and babies, weddings and showers, and— *Showers!*

Angela dropped back down onto the bench seat. She would have to give Leigh a bridal shower. There was no way out of that. Leigh was her best friend and it would be expected by everyone. How would she ever endure the sight of the filmy underthings that were sure to be presented to her friend?

Angela drew a deep breath and rose to her feet again. She'd had more than enough of weddings and brides for one day. She checked her wallet for change, then headed toward the telephone to call a cab. She had other shopping to do, and it was exactly what she needed to change the tone of her day.

"You know, I've heard you can tell a lot about a person from the items they put in their grocery cart."

Angela's heart made an odd little skip. She grabbed one of the packages on the shelf in front of her and turned around.

Hosea Stevens smiled and lifted a package of adhesive from her wire basket. "For instance…you have false teeth." He dropped the package and picked up a small packet of batteries for hearing aids. "You're hard of hearing and—" he waved a ten-pack of acid reducers through the air "—you obviously suffer from severe indigestion." He grinned and pointed to the carton of special drink for senior citizens in the bottom of the cart. "Maybe it would help that problem if you let up on that stuff."

Angela laughed in spite of the fluttering butterflies

suddenly trapped in her stomach. She held aloft the package of corn pads in her hand. "Hello, Pastor Stevens. Have you a comment on these?"

"Hello, Angela Warren. Nary a one—they're self-evident. But I do have a question." He fell into step beside her as she started pushing her shopping cart down the aisle. "Why all the geriatric products?"

"They're for some of the folks at Pine Glen." Angela stopped the cart and reached for a package of cookies that were on the back of the top shelf. She went on tiptoe but couldn't quite reach.

"Here...let me." Hosea's hand brushed against hers as he reached for the cookies. Angela jerked back so quickly she bumped into him. His free arm closed around her shoulders. "Whoa! Steady there." He let go of her and tossed the cookies into the cart. "Do you go there often?"

"What? Where? Oh—Pine Glen." Angela turned and scanned the shelves on the opposite side of the aisle to hide her discomposure. Her heart raced. Her pulse pounded. *Get hold of yourself!* she ordered fiercely. *It was an accident. He didn't mean to touch you.* She forced a calm, polite tone into her voice. "I try to go at least twice a week—usually Wednesday evening and Sunday afternoon."

She crossed the aisle and picked up a package of cinnamon crackers. Thinking about other things always helped to master the fear.

"So they all place their orders for special items with you, is that it?"

"No. They would never do that." Angela shook her head, laid the crackers on top of the drink carton and went back for a second package. Her heart slowed. Her pulse returned to normal. "They're all very careful not to take advantage. But I can't help noticing the little things they need when I'm around them."

"Like cookies and cinnamon crackers?"

There was a teasing note in his voice. Angela looked up and met, full force, the warmth in Hosea's eyes. Her heart started sprinting again. She dropped her gaze to the cart before he could read the answering warmth that was spreading through her.

Dear heaven, what was happening to her?

She cleared her throat. "Sophie hasn't been eating well lately, and these cookies are her favorites. I thought— Oh! I almost forgot."

"What?"

"The coloring book and crayons." Angela reached for the handle of the cart at the same moment Hosea did. His hand closed over hers. She yanked hers away.

"Sorry." His knuckles whitened on the handle. "Why don't I push this thing while you lead. I want to hear about this coloring book. That certainly doesn't fit it with the other items you've got."

Angela nodded and turned away. *Lord, please help me. Please make him leave.*

She tried for a deep breath, failed and started walking up the next aisle. "It's nothing really. Last week I overheard Sophie telling Margaret that she loved to color, but had never had a coloring book and crayons of her own."

She stopped in front of the colorful display of coloring books, selected one with pictures of young girls in old-fashioned clothing and riffled through the pages.

It calmed her. She stared down at the lace-ruffled mob-caps, the pantalettes, and thought about Sophie. "She said she always had to share with her brothers and sisters and never got to color the first page."

Angela closed the book and put it in the cart. "I suppose it's silly of me to get her one. But she's ninety-four and...well...there's no time like the present."

What a thing to say to a pastor! Angela's cheeks warmed. She took the book back out of the cart. "I'm being silly. I shouldn't get it. It's such a little thing and—"

"Not when you've never had one." Hosea's hand closed over hers on the book. "Put it back in the cart, Angela. It's not silly at all. It's kind...and compassionate...and wonderful."

So was the look in his eyes. And, surprisingly, the touch of his hand. Angela waited for the rush of fear and repulsion a man's touch always engendered in her, but there was only a strange, tingling warmth. Her heart thudded. That *had* been a fear response she'd felt earlier, hadn't it? *Hadn't it?*

Angela slid her hand away from his touch. This was getting more than a little alarming. She dropped the book into the cart, grabbed a large, deluxe box of crayons and added them to the pile. "Well, that's everything."

She gathered her courage, glanced up at Hosea and reached for the cart handle. "It's been nice talking with you, Pastor. Thank you for pushing the cart. I'll just—" She stopped with her hand stretched out in midair as he shook his head.

"These things are too heavy for you to carry. I'll help you take them to your car."

Angela stared at him, then looked down at the small gifts that had suddenly become a trap, while her mind raced about searching for a way of escape. "That's very thoughtful of you, Pastor, but, you see, I—"

"Is something wrong? Is there someone—? Oh. Well…that was presumptuous of me, wasn't it?" Hosea frowned and stepped back from the cart. "I'm sorry, Angela. I certainly didn't mean to interfere if there's someone with you."

"Oh, no, Pastor, it's nothing like that. I'm quite alone."

Always and ever alone! The hateful thought made her cringe. Angela took hold of the cart handle and forced a polite smile. "It's only that I don't have my car with me. I'm calling a cab, and there will be a delay until it arrives."

"Is that all! Well, that's no problem. I'll just load these things into my car and take you home."

Angela's eyes widened. He had sounded relived. As if— Oh dear heaven! He couldn't be seriously attracted to her. Could he?

Angela tightened her grip on the cart handle and tried, desperately, to think of an excuse to get away. *Lord, help me! What can I do?*

Of course! Relief surged through her as the answer slid smoothly into her mind. "Thank you anyway, Pastor, but I'm not going home. I'm going to Pine Glen."

"Even better."

Angela's hands fell from the cart handle.

Hosea smiled and took possession of the cart. "I've been meaning to go out there and introduce myself—see if I might minister to the residents in some way. This gives me the perfect opportunity."

He wheeled the cart around the corner and headed for the checkout counters. "Ah! An open aisle."

Feeling helpless, confused and just a tad betrayed, Angela moved forward into the narrow space and began unloading the cart.

Chapter Nine

"This way, Pastor Stevens. We'll put the— Oh, listen!"

Hosea focused his attention on the sound in the distance. "Someone is playing a mean piano."

"It's Sophie. She must be feeling better."

"The coloring book Sophie?"

"Yes."

Angela looked up at him and smiled. Hosea was suddenly thankful for the grocery bags he held in his arms. He wanted to touch her. Hold her. He wrenched his mind away from the dangerous path it had started down and shifted his grip on the bags as an excuse to look away. "She's a talented lady."

"Oh, she is! She used to play in a piano bar in the 'good old days.'" Angela looked back over her shoulder at him as they turned down a wide hall. "She has some wild stories."

"I'll bet." Hosea loosened the death hold he had

on the bags before he crushed the cookies. "Maybe I'll get to hear some of them someday."

"I'm sure you will. Everyone here loves to talk about the past. And they all have interesting tales to tell." They stepped through a high archway. "Let's get rid of these things before our arms go numb, and I'll introduce you to everyone."

"I'd appreciate that." Hosea took note of the Office sign on the door to his left and fell into step beside her. "Have you been coming here long?"

"About two years."

He followed her across a large room to a semicircular counter that hid desks and various pieces of office equipment.

Angela plunked down the bag she was carrying. "Hello, Terri. I'd like you to meet Pastor Stevens. Pastor Stevens…Mrs. Bellows. She's the RN in charge at night."

"Hello, Mrs. Bellows."

"Hello, Pastor Stevens." The RN smiled and nodded toward the bags in Hosea's arms. "I see Angela has pressed you into service carrying her goodies for her. You can just leave them here on the counter. The aides will take care of them."

She peeked into one of the bags he set down. "Anything special this time, Angela?"

"A package of corn pads for Prudence. And these are for Sophie." Angela pulled the coloring book and crayons from the bag in front of her. "I'll just put them in her room."

"Why don't I do that for you?" The nurse smiled at Angela and held out her hand. "I know you don't want to miss Sophie's concert, and she's been playing awhile already.''

"Thanks, Terri." Angela handed over the items. "I do want to introduce Pastor Stevens to the others, and a gathering like this is the perfect opportunity. Perhaps we'll see you lat—''

Bells clanged.

"Oops. That's probably Mr. Thomas trying to get out again. Bye.'' The nurse spun about and hurried down a hallway behind her as a second set of bells went off.

Hosea stared after her. ''What's that all about?''

"Billy Thomas loves to go outside, but he suffers from Alzheimer's and he'll get lost if he goes out without an aide. They have an alarm system that rings when anyone with Alzheimer's goes through the inside set of doors.''

"I see. Are there many people here with Alzheimer's?''

"A few.'' Angela led him toward an archway on their left. "It's so frightening for those in the earlier stages to realize they are losing control of their minds.''

Angela paused beside the archway and Hosea studied her as she swept her gaze over the elderly people seated in the large room beyond. Her expression was soft, her eyes warm with compassion. When she glanced back up at him, he sucked in his breath and jammed his hands into his pockets.

"Every time I come here I pray for God's love and peace to suffuse these people and drive out all fear. And for Jesus to save all those who have not yet surrendered their lives to him before it's too late and they are lost forever.'' Her voice broke. She looked away. ''He's the only one that can penetrate their confusion with his truth.''

Suddenly she bit down on her lip. Her cheeks flushed. She looked embarrassed and utterly adorable. Her gaze sought his. Hosea's heart gave a little kick, and picked up its beat.

''I'm sorry, Pastor. You know all that far better than I. Sometimes I get carried away when I talk about the Lord.''

Before he could respond, she whirled about and stepped through the archway. Immediately, people began smiling and waving, calling her name, and motioning for her to sit beside them. It was clear they all loved her.

Hosea watched the scene for a moment, marveling at the change God had worked in Angela. She was truly a woman of God. She bore no trace of the frightened young prostitute he'd prayed for six years ago. He smiled and followed her into the room, his heart filled with a music more marvelous and lasting than any the talented woman at the piano could ever play.

One by one song requests were shouted out by the people gathered in the room and the nimble fingers of the small, gray-haired woman seated at the piano danced over the keys as she complied. At last she held up one hand, then lowered it and played ''Good Night, Ladies.''

The requests stopped. A parade of wheelchairs, walkers and people leaning on canes formed and headed for the archway. Angela rose and moved slowly from person to person dispensing hugs, exchanging jokes, and introducing Hosea. They reached the piano as the last person was wheeled from the room by one of the aides.

"Sophie, that was wonderful." Angela gave the little woman a hug, then straightened and indicated the man at her side. "Sophie, I'd like you to meet Pastor Hosea Stevens. Pastor Stevens…Sophie Winslow."

Hosea smiled down into the woman's intelligent, assessing gaze. "Hello, Sophie Winslow. I enjoyed your concert. I can't say I knew all the songs—but I play a little myself, so I know you played them well."

"Not as well as I used to. My fingers aren't as limber as they once were." Sophie tipped her head to one side and gave Hosea a coy smile. "But I can still coax a tune from the keys."

"And a compliment from an appreciative listener?" Hosea grinned down at the little woman. "You're terrific on that piano and you know it."

Sophie laughed. "All right—I know it. But it's still nice to hear. A woman my age doesn't get many compliments."

Hosea skimmed his gaze over her upturned face. Age had taken its toll, but there was still a vestige of what must have once been an exceptional beauty. "I imagine you've had your share of compliments, Miss Sophie."

"Right again." Sophie chuckled and patted Angela's arm. "I like your young man, dear—he's got a nice sense of humor. Bring him by to see me again." She reached for her cane and glanced at Hosea. "Forgive me, Pastor Stevens, I don't mean to be rude, but at my age, when you get tired—you get tired. I'm going to my room and rest. Good evening.''

''Good evening, Miss Sophie.'' Hosea took hold of the elderly woman's free hand. ''It was a pleasure meeting you. And with your permission, I will call again. But—to set the record straight—Angela didn't ask me here this evening. I sort of pushed my way in this time. I'm not her young man.''

''Really?'' The old woman swept her gaze to Angela, then looked back at Hosea and snorted. ''You could have fooled me.'' She gave him a sly look. ''Then again, it might be yourself you're fooling. Time will tell.'' She handed him her cane and trailed her fingers over the piano keys. A lovely old-fashioned melody filled the room. When she finished playing, she took back her cane and pushed to her feet. ''That was for you, Pastor. Now, goodbye.''

She turned to give Angela a hug. ''Goodbye, dear. And thank you. I've been sleeping so well since we had our little talk a few weeks ago.'' She started toward the door.

''Miss Sophie?'' Hosea smiled. ''That tune you played for me was lovely, but I'm not familiar with it. Would you tell me the name of it?''

She gave him a cheeky smile. ''It's called, 'Let Me Call You Sweetheart.' You might want to learn the words, Pastor. There's nothing like a song to express your feelings.'' With a dry little chuckle she turned and walked out of the room.

Angela went hot with embarrassment. *Lord, may the floor open up, swallow me and close over my head!* It didn't even crack a little. She glanced down and sighed. "Pastor Stevens, I'm so sorry, I—"

"Angela, I apologize for—"

They stopped, looked at each other and burst into laughter.

"Pastor, I am truly sorry. I don't know whatever possessed Sophie to say such a thing."

"There's no need to apologize, Angela." Hosea grinned down at her as they walked from the room. "My grandparents are in their seventies, so I'm used to this sort of thing. My grandfather made my teenage years a horror of embarrassment. I thought I would never live through them. Now, they are some of my funniest, fondest memories...and greatest lessons."

He slanted a glance down at her as they walked to the exit. "If there is any apology due, it is mine to you." He grinned again, and opened the door for her. "As I said, I'm experienced with elderly people, and you may be in for a good deal of good-natured teasing because I accompanied you here tonight."

"I'll live through it." Angela climbed into the car and gave him a rueful smile. "I think."

Hosea laughed, closed her door, and walked around to his own side. Angela watched him back out of the parking space and pull out onto the highway. He had a nice laugh. And nice hands. They looked strong and competent. But their touch was gentle.

She swept her gaze upward. He was certainly handsome. With his tanned skin, blue eyes, and sun-bleached, dark-blond hair he looked more the athlete than—

"Is there anywhere else you need to go, Angela?"

He flashed her a quick smile. "My car is at your command."

He had caught her staring at him! Angela snapped her gaze straight ahead. "That's very kind, Pastor Stevens, but I've nothing else pressing, so it's, 'Home, James.'"

"The name's Hosea, ma'am." He glanced her way. "I mean that, Angela. I'd like you to call me Hosea if it wouldn't make you uncomfortable. Being called Pastor Stevens all the time makes me feel one-dimensional—as if I should be constantly preaching."

She looked over at him to answer and promptly forgot what she was going to say. She'd never noticed that little scar at the corner of his right eye before. It was just where those tiny crinkles formed when he smiled....

"You don't want me to start preaching, do you?"

He gave her a crooked grin that made her toes tingle. Angela pulled her attention from his mouth and focused on his words. "I wouldn't mind. You're a good preacher. I get a lot out of your sermons."

"That's good to hear." His gaze touched hers, and suddenly her lungs felt too small for the air in them. "But about the name?"

"Hosea it is—in private."

"Yes—in private. Thank you." He relaxed back against the seat.

Angela stared at him a moment, then dragged her gaze back to the road. She didn't feel relaxed, she felt...edgy. "If you need to stop at the grocery store on the way to my house, I don't mind. After all, it was my fault you didn't get whatever it was you were after. And it would be out of your way for you to take me home and then return to the store.''

''That's thoughtful of you, but I was only shopping for dinner and I'd rather go to a restaurant if you would be so kind as to join me. You see…'' He leaned a little her way and lowered his voice. ''Can you keep a secret?''

Angela shot him a look. ''Yes, of course I can, but—''

''I'm on my own for the week. Mrs. Thompson was called out of town on a family emergency and I've no one to cook for me. That's why I was in the grocery store. I was going to buy some frozen dinners to tide me over the dry spell.''

''Frozen dinners? Why? All you have to do is make it known Hilda is gone and—''

''The ladies of the church will be happy to supply my meals. I know. But they're the reason I want my solitude kept secret, even though they mean well. If my news gets out, I will be buried in food. Every woman in the church will bring her prize recipe in a casserole large enough for a family of ten. And while I like to eat as much, or better, than the next man, I'm only one person. And a man can stand only so much tuna or green-bean casserole.'' He gave an exaggerated shudder.

Angela laughed. ''You'd better not let Emily Evans hear you say that. Her Noodle-Tuna Delight is her pride.''

''That's just what I'm talking about.'' Hosea grinned. ''Let me see if I can guess…extra mushrooms and potato chip topping?''

''Nope. That's Francine Burrows.''

"Hmm. Peas, celery and carrots?"

She grinned and shook her head. "That's uncanny—but wrong. That's Thelma Fisher."

Hosea knit his dark-brown brows together in an expression of fierce concentration. "I've got it! Chick peas and garlic."

Angela's mouth gaped open. "You're joking."

"Nope. I've eaten it."

"Well, I can't even imagine that! Anyway, you didn't guess. Emily is chives, cheese and croutons."

"Ah, yes."

"I don't believe it." She fixed a suspicious look on him. "You've had that combination also?"

He laughed and nodded. "All pastors are noodle-tuna combination experts. So what do you say?" He fastened his gaze on hers briefly before turning back to the road. "Will you take pity on me, keep my secret and have dinner with me tonight?"

Angela pressed her hands over the sudden flutter in her stomach and took a deep breath to refuse. "After a horror story like that one, how can I say no?" Her heart jolted. *What had she said?*

Hosea nodded. "Good. How about The River House? I haven't had opportunity to eat there yet, but I've heard they have great food."

"Yes. It's a very good menu." Angela stared blindly at the oncoming traffic. How had that yes come out when she had meant to say no? She forced the light note back into her voice. "And there's nary a noodle-tuna entree to be found on it."

Hosea chuckled. "Bless them, that settles it, The River House it is." He checked his mirror, pulled over into the left-hand lane and prepared to turn onto Hillman Boulevard.

"Well, The River House gets four stars for its menu as far as I'm concerned—and two more for its location. What a terrific idea to join their garden walkway to the Riverside Park path." Hosea grinned down at Angela. "I don't know about you, but I need to walk off some of that excellent dinner…not to mention the dessert."

She laughed up at him. "I warned you about that chocolate cake."

Hosea's grin widened. "Yes, you did. And you were right. But every bite of it was worth an hour or so of exercise." He put his hand on the small of her back and guided her onto the Riverside Park footbridge. "Just look at those stars! I love the town of Harmony. And the park has become one of my favorite places. I often drive out here late at night and run on the path along the river. There's something about the soft ripple of flowing water that's great for unwinding tangled thoughts and clearing your mind."

He glanced over his shoulder at the softly lit gardens that led back to the restaurant. "A place like this could never exist in the city. At least not without glaring streetlights and security guards everywhere."

Angela tensed. It made her uneasy whenever he made reference to the city. She gave an inward sigh of relief when he removed his hand and stepped to the railing to look down at the water. Talk about tangled thoughts and hopelessly knotted emotions! She shouldn't even be here with him. Every moment in his presence put her life in Harmony in jeopardy. And now, with all these new feelings…

She glanced at Hosea's back and moved slowly forward. Maybe *she* should start running. Maybe she should start running right now. The distance that would put between herself and this intelligent, good-humored, and altogether too charming man would definitely help to straighten out her—

"I've been wondering about something, Angela."

She stopped dead in her tracks as her mind instantly flashed to her past. "Oh?" She forced herself to turn around. He was leaning against the railing looking at her.

"Is Sophie born again?"

Angela stiffened. This was dangerous ground. She loved the term born again, it brought back the moment she had first experienced God's love for her, and the wondrous changes His love had worked in her life—but it was the last thing she wanted to discuss with Hosea Stevens.

Angela yanked her thoughts away from the past. "Yes, Sophie has accepted the Lord as her Savior." *Please, Lord! Please don't let him remember! Please don't let those words—*

"I thought so." Hosea straightened. "You led her to the Lord recently, didn't you?"

Angela nodded, watching him carefully. "Yes. A few weeks ago. How did you know?"

"That comment she made about being able to sleep well ever since you had a conversation with her—that speaks of peace. And I know of only one source for that kind of peace."

He left the railing and stepped to her side. "Isn't it a wonderful feeling knowing someone is safe in Jesus' arms for all eternity because you shared the truth of His love with them?

Angela couldn't speak. Fear captured her voice. Was he talking about Sophie? Or was he talking about the night he had led her to Jesus? Had he remembered? She began to shiver. She didn't want him to remember. And suddenly it had nothing to do with the havoc that would wreak in her life. Suddenly it had to do with the man. With the way he looked, and talked, and smiled and— *Oh, Lord, I'm so afraid!*

"Angela?"

When had she closed her eyes? She opened them and looked directly into Hosea's steady gaze. In spite of her fear, something came alive deep in her heart. A soft warmth stole throughout her body. Her knees threatened to buckle. There was such gentleness in his eyes. Such warmth and caring. Such—

Angela's fear erupted into full-blown panic. She took a step backward. *Oh, Dear God, help me. Help me! Protect my heart, Lord.*

"Well, hello, you two."

Leigh! Angela whipped around as her friend walked onto the bridge. Relief surged through her.

Hosea stepped in front of her. "Hello yourself, Dr. Roberts. Where's the other half of you?"

Angela ducked behind Hosea's broad shoulders and made an effort to gather herself together. She was in no shape to face Leigh's discerning doctor's eyes.

"Phil's in his office—fighting with an archway that doesn't want to go in the location he designed for it."

Angela saw a fall of red hair beyond the edge of Hosea's arm as Leigh tilted her head to the side.

Hosea lifted his hand and rubbed at the back of his neck, blocking off her view. "And what brings you here on this lovely evening?"

Leigh laughed. "Where else would I go to walk off some of the stiffness from performing a long, difficult delivery? This is the only park in town."

Hosea was distracting Leigh! Had he guessed her emotions were in turmoil? Did he know how he made her feel? Angela sucked in air. She couldn't let that happen. She pasted a smile on her face and stepped to the side.

"Hi, Leigh. How did the delivery turn out?

"Couldn't be better. You have two, tiny new neighbors."

"Two! Mrs. Fullerton had twins?"

"Yep. Five and a half pounds of them—total."

Angela winced inwardly as Leigh's gaze scanned her face. She kept her smile firmly in place.

"Angela, are you—?"

"That's pretty small, isn't it? Are they all right?"

Leigh's left eyebrow lifted at Hosea's interruption. She gave him a long, searching look, and Angela knew her friend had gone on point. She could almost hear her sniffing the air.

"They're holding their own. The smallest one is having some trouble breathing, but I think she's going to make it. Dr. Fields is the best pediatrician around and he's taking care of them—as is the Lord."

She gave Hosea a tired smile. "That's one of the best parts of my job. My hands are the first to be laid on those tiny new lives, and I say a prayer for salvation for every one of them.'' Her smile widened. ''That way I have a share in their natural birth and their spiritual birth.''

''Now there's a rare privilege. I've never thought about the laying on of hands in quite that way before.'' Hosea smiled. ''Those babies are very fortunate to have you orchestrating their arrival into this world.''

''They are indeed—she said modestly.'' Leigh laughed, then leaned against the railing, pulled off her loafer and rubbed her foot. ''I think this walking thing was a mistake.'' She slipped her shoe back on and straightened. ''I'm going to go home, light a dozen lavender candles and soak the stiffness away in an herbal bath.''

She turned toward Angela. ''Thanks again for today, pal. Phil was thrilled to death when I told him. I've been a real bear over this gown thing. But don't tell him I admitted it.''

She slid her gaze to Hosea, then back to Angela and smiled. ''I'll give you a call tomorrow when I'm not so tired and we'll talk. Bye.''

Angela's stomach flopped. How was she to deal with Leigh? She was so discerning that—

''Gown thing?''

Angela looked up. Hosea's gaze skimmed over her face, dropped to her mouth. Her pulse quickened. She picked a bright-red leaf that had fallen from a nearby maple tree off the railing and studied it's delicate veining. ''It's nothing. Leigh's been in a muddle over choosing a wedding gown. I went shopping with her today and helped her pick one out.'' She glanced up at him. "That's why I didn't have my car at the grocery store. Leigh got paged."

"I see." He lifted his gaze from her mouth. She nearly lost control at the look in his dark-blue eyes. She looked away.

Hosea stepped back. Cleared his throat. "Well, I'm sorry Leigh was having a difficult time. And I'm very sorry if I'm going to be the cause of future discomfort for you with the Pine Glen residents. But I can't find it in my heart to be sorry for tonight." He smiled down at her. "It worked out very well for me. I had a lovely companion for dinner…and I didn't have to eat any noodle-tuna casserole."

He gestured toward the other end of the bridge. "Shall we continue our walk?"

She wanted to. With all her heart she wanted to be with him—and that terrified her. She shook her head. "I'm sorry. It's getting late, and I've an early presentation to make tomorrow. If you don't mind, I'd like to go home now."

Angela stared down at the leaf in her hand, acutely aware of Hosea, and of a sudden, desperate desire to step into his arms, to feel their strength close about her. *Oh, God! Oh God! Why did You let this happen to me?* She closed her eyes and drew a deep breath to calm her pounding, racing heart.

"All right. It seems a shame to waste this beautiful evening, but I understand."

Did he? She hoped not. Angela took another breath and opened her eyes. The leaf was shaking. She dropped it over the railing.

"Perhaps another time."

He knew. The truth was there in his eyes. He had seen straight through the barrier she had raised to her traitorous heart. Angela's lungs stopped working. She nodded her head, then turned to watch the softly flowing water carry the leaf away. Tears filled her eyes. ''Perhaps.''

It was a lie. She didn't dare let it happen again. She blinked the tears from her eyes, straightened her shoulders, and walked off the bridge.

Hosea picked up his pen and absently doodled on his notepad as he sat in his dark office, staring out the window. Thoughts whirled around in his mind like a tornado, but one stood out from the rest. It was becoming increasingly difficult for him to separate his pastoral care of Angela from his growing personal feelings for her.

Oh, if only the Lord would speak. The indecision is agony.

Hosea gave a scornful snort, threw down the pen and scrubbed his cheeks and neck with his hands. Who was he kidding? He loved Angela. There was no indecision. His heart already knew. The agony was caused by uncertainty of God's will. He thought he knew it—but he couldn't trust himself to hear right, to interpret the signs that would lead him on the path he was to follow.

A low groan rose from Hosea's heart and escaped his lips. ''Lord, help me! Your word says a man's heart is deceitful above all things. That You alone can know it. I dare not trust my heart in this, Lord. I've pledged my life to serving You—to caring for Your children, and I don't want to do anything to endanger that. I need You to speak clearly, in a way I can not misinterpret, because, I confess, I want Your answer to be yes. I want Angela for my bride. I want to share my life with her. Nonetheless, Lord…'' he forced himself to say the words ''…Thy will be done.''

Pain shot through him. Would he have to give her up for the sake of his ministry?

Hosea buried his head in his hands, praying, and waiting for the turmoil in his heart to cease—waiting, for the words he had spoken to become truth. When the battle between his flesh and spirit was over—when he had yielded his will wholly to the Lord's—he felt as wrung out and depleted as if he had just run a marathon.

He lifted his head and leaned back, staring into the surrounding darkness. The only light visible was the cool, silver moonlight coming in the window, and a thin gold sliver that sneaked through the crack under his office door. He glanced that way. *How bright that little sliver of light is in the darkness, Lord. Just like the light of truth You shine into the darkness of our lives. Thank You for Your truth.*

Hosea blew out a gust of air and turned on his desk lamp. Time to do some work. There was no sense in going home. He sure wouldn't be able to sleep for a while. He reached for his pen and his gaze fell on his notepad. Scattered randomly over the page, formed by the aimless shapes and squiggles of his doodling, yet clearly visible and in order, were the letters of his name, and the numbers, two and nineteen.

His breath caught. That was clear enough. And it

certainly fit. But was it God? His momentary exhilaration died. He knew the story of the prophet Hosea well. As impossible as it seemed, had he somehow, subconsciously, been able to make those letters and numbers out of his doodling? How could he know? How could he ever be sure?

Hosea dropped the notepad onto his desk and plowed his hands through his hair. This whole thing was driving him crazy! What was the verse? He knew the story of Hosea, but he couldn't say what chapter two, verse nineteen was—not off the top of his head.

He went to reach for his Bible. It wasn't there. He'd left his Bible in the car! He plunked down into his chair, yanked open the bottom desk drawer and pulled out the Bible he had used when he first started preaching. There was a folded paper tucked between the pages. Of their own volition, his trained fingers opened to the page and removed the marker.

A shivery tingle started at the tip of his spine and spread throughout Hosea's body as he stared down at the yellowing Crossroads Church bulletin he held in his hands. He glanced at the place it had marked in his old Bible for six years—Hosea, chapter two. His pulse raced. He skimmed his gaze down the page and read verse nineteen. "I will betroth you to me forever: I will betroth you in righteousness and justice, in love and compassion. I will betroth you in faithfulness…"

His whoop hurt his ears. It echoed off the office walls.

Hosea leaped from his seat and raced down the hallway, laughing like a maniac. He knew it didn't matter, but, right now, he couldn't bear having a roof between him and His Heavenly Father. He shoved through the door leading to the parking lot, leaped off the steps and spun around, raising his hands toward the night sky. "Hallelujah! Thank You, Lord! Thank You, Father! I praise Your holy name!"

He could have sworn the moon smiled and every single star winked at him. He winked back, then stood staring up at the sky, awed by God's love. After a moment, he turned and went inside. He had a phone call to make.

"Hello?"

"Mom? It's Hosea. Get Dad on the other phone." The grin that split his face made it hard for him to form his words. "I have good news. I have God's answer! And, when the time is right, I'm going to ask Angela to marry me."

Chapter Ten

"No."

"But, Leigh—?"

"No, Angela! I'm too busy. I can't fit one more thing into my schedule before the wedding. Besides, you're already doing more than enough for me. No shower." Leigh dipped her fingertip into the bowl of caramel icing Angela was drizzling on the toasted hazelnut torte she had made for the Sunday school director's farewell dinner, licked it off and rolled her eyes. "Yum! That's wonderful!"

Angela gave her a look.

"What?" Leigh grinned at her. "I'm a doctor. My hands are always clean."

Angela laughed and shook her head. "You're incorrigible!"

"I know. I'm also going to be late for my fitting if I don't run." Leigh grabbed her coat.

"Wait a minute, Leigh—I need a favor."

Leigh stopped shrugging into her coat and gave Angela an assessing glance. "Uh-oh. I don't like that don't-ask-questions-about-this tone of voice. You've been using it a lot lately. What's the favor?"

"Would you please take this cake to the supper for me?"

"You're not coming?"

"No."

"Why not?" Leigh sighed. "Now your face has that closed look that matches your don't-ask-questions-about-this tone of voice. What's going on, Angela? Why won't you come?"

Angela held her silence.

Leigh changed her tactic. "Will you come if I beg?"

"Don't, Leigh." Angela blinked away the sudden blur caused by the moisture that sprang to her eyes and turned back to the cake. Leigh dropped her coat onto a chair, reached over and took the fork from her hand.

"Sit down, Angela. We're going to talk."

"Leigh—"

"Sit down." It was her doctor's voice that brooked no argument. Angela dropped into a chair.

Leigh took her own seat and leaned forward. "Listen to me, Angela—I'm a doctor. I notice things about people. I'm trained to recognize signs of stress, unhappiness and pain." Her voice softened. "You've got them all, friend—and they're getting worse. Let me help you. Please. Talk to me. Whatever the problem is, it won't get better if you hold it inside. It will just fester and grow and make you sick."

She reached out and covered Angela's tightly

clasped hands with her own. "You know I'm right, Angela. Tell me what's wrong. Let's work it out together."

Oh, if only that was possible! Angela's throat tightened. She met the plea with more silence.

Leigh sighed and leaned back against her chair. "Well, at least you're not denying there's a problem. That's a start. We'll go on from there."

"No, we won't. You have to stop—"

Leigh shook her head. "I'm not going to be silent, Angela. I've been silent too long. You're not sleeping well—"

Angela started to speak, then stopped as her friend held up a restraining hand.

"—as testified to by those lavender circles of fatigue under your eyes. You're not eating right. I'd judge you've lost about five pounds in the last few weeks, which, by the way, you can ill afford. You're avoiding all church meetings and activities. And you hurry in and out of services as if the building is on fire."

Leigh drew a deep breath and leaned forward again. "You don't have to say anything, Angela. I'd have to be deaf, dumb and blind not to know this is about Hosea. And notice, I didn't say Pastor Stevens. That was on purpose. Because this isn't about Hosea Stevens, the pastor...this is about Hosea Stevens, the man."

Angela surged to her feet. Her chair tipped over and scraped the wall. She ignored it. "This is about me, Leigh. And *only* me. You leave Hosea out of it. *I'm* the one with the problem. And that is all I am going to say on the subject, now…or ever. I hope you value our friendship enough to respect my wishes in the matter.''

Shock rippled across Leigh's face. Angela pressed a hand to her chest and struggled to catch a breath. Her vision blurred. Leigh's hand closed around hers.

''Angela, what's wrong? What's causing you such pain?''

She shook her head, fighting back the urge to throw herself into Leigh's arms and sob out the truth. ''You're the best friend I've ever had, or could ever want, Leigh. But there are some things I just can't talk about—not even to you. So, please…*please*…don't press me.''

Angela snatched up the icing bowl and hurried to the sink. Over the sound of the running water she could hear Leigh rise to her feet and put on her coat. She braced herself as the sound of her friend's footsteps crossed the kitchen.

''You forgot this.''

A fork covered with caramel icing appeared before her. ''Thanks.'' Angela glanced up and met Leigh's gaze. She swallowed hard and turned back to scrubbing the bowl.

''We could use you in surgery, Angela. The way you're going at that dish there isn't going to be any color left on it. So—as a doctor—I recommend you just stick it in the dishwasher.''

Angela snatched her hands out of the sink.

Leigh grinned. ''I told you I notice things, compadre.'' She gave Angela a quick hug, then walked over and opened the door. ''Tell you what—I'll be back to pick up the cake at six. I don't like it. But I'll do it. And, meanwhile, Angela…I'll be praying. God's wisdom is perfect. And He has an answer for everything.''

· The door clicked closed.

God's wisdom is perfect. And He has an answer for everything.

Leigh's words hung in the air—pressed the breath from Angela's lungs. ''…be sure your sin will find you out.'' Thought of the exposure the scripture verse spoke of terrified her.

After six years God had brought her face-to-face with her past. And with God, she had nowhere to hide.

''Wow!''

''I told you.'' Leigh grinned at Hosea.

''This is fantastic!'' Hosea forked up another bite of the cake and made a manful effort not to smack his lips when he finished chewing. ''Who made it?''

''Angela.''

Hosea's hand froze in midair. He recovered quickly and finished lifting the next bite of cake to his mouth—but not quickly enough. Leigh had noticed. Those doctor's eyes of hers never missed a thing. To her credit she didn't so much as smile.

Hosea laid down his fork and poured cream into his cup of coffee. ''I guess I missed her.'' He fought back the urge to jump up and run out to the parking lot to see if she was still there. ''I didn't think she was here.''

''She wasn't. I brought the cake for her.''

''I see.'' He couldn't quite keep the disappointment from his voice.

Leigh locked her gaze on his. "She's a wonderful cook. I have wild dreams of hiring her when Phil and I get rich and can afford someone of her talent."

"Talent? Whose talent? In what area? Who are we hiring?" Phil slid a paper plate with a brownie on it onto the table, and dropped into the chair beside Leigh.

"Angela, hon. To do our cooking and baking." Leigh smiled and slid a piece of the hazelnut torte she had been saving toward him. "You might want to trade that brownie in for this."

"You angel!" Phil shoved the brownie aside and kissed Leigh's cheek. "Jeff Archer waylaid me with a question, and by the time I got to the dessert table the cake was all gone." He took a bite, licked a spot of icing from his lip, and grinned. "Yep! Just as delicious as I expected. It's a good thing Angela isn't interested in marriage or— Ow!"

"Oh…I'm sorry." Leigh gave Phil a look that could have withered a tree. "Was that your foot?"

"It used to be." Phil shot her a what-was-that-for? glance and leaned down to rub his foot.

Hosea chuckled.

"Pastor Stevens?"

He lifted his head and looked up at Walter Foster.

"Sorry to interrupt, but it's that time."

"Okay. Thanks, Allen. I'll be right there."

Hosea wiped his mouth with his napkin, rose to his feet, then leaned across the table and lowered his voice so only Leigh could hear him. "It's all in God's hands, Leigh. But it's nice to know I have an ally. Still, you don't have to maim the man—I don't discourage easily.''

Leigh's mouth gaped open.

Hosea gave her a broad wink, then turned and walked to the front of the room to open the evening's special program.

''Thank you for the poinsettia, dear. It's lovely. Now, stop fussing with it and come over here and talk to me.''

''I didn't realize I was fussing.'' Angela tucked in a loose corner of the red foil that covered the poinsettia's container, then went over and sat on the edge of Sophie's bed. ''What do you want to talk about?''

''Your young man for starters. He came to see me the other day. We had a nice long chat about the Lord. And then I asked him why he hadn't been here with you.''

''Oh, Sophie! I wish you hadn't.''

The elderly woman ignored her.

''He said he didn't see you very often. And his eyes had the same sadness I see in your eyes right now. But his weren't troubled.''

Angela started to her feet. Sophie reached out and grabbed her hand.

''Why don't you tell me what's wrong, dear? Maybe I can help. I haven't lived all these years without learning a thing or two about the vicissitudes of life.''

''That's very kind, Sophie, but—''

''I'm not being kind, Angela! I care about you. And

I don't like seeing you unhappy. Now tell me what's wrong. Did you two have an argument?''

"No, of course not." Angela forced a smile and tried for a light note. "You don't argue with your pastor."

"I'm not talking about your pastor. I'm talking about your young man."

"Hosea Stevens is *not* my young man!" The force of her response startled her. "I'm sorry, Sophie. I didn't mean to—"

"He'd like to be."

Heavens! She was worse than Leigh. Angela rose from the bed, wrapped her arms around herself and walked over to look out the window. "You're mistaken."

"No, dear, I'm not. The man's in lo—"

Angela whirled about. "I don't want to hear anymore, Sophie! Please. Let's talk about something else."

The old woman stared at her for a moment, then nodded. "All right, dear. I'll say no more about Hosea." She pushed the button to lower the head of her bed a little and leaned back. "How is that girl…? What's her name? Cathy? Yes, that's it…Cathy. How is she doing at college?"

Angela released her pent-up breath. "Cathy's doing fine." She stepped to the bed. "Sophie, please forgive me. I didn't mean to be sharp with you."

"I know, dear." Sophie patted Angela's hand and smiled. "Don't give it another thought. Did they tell you at the desk about the Thanksgiving goings-on they have planned?"

"No. I came straight to your room." Angela perched on the arm of the reclining chair beside the bed. "What do they have planned?"

"Well, first we are going to be treated to a parade of pilgrims, Native Americans and turkeys. The first four grades of Wilson Elementary School have made costumes and we are going to vote on the best in each category. Then, they are going to put on a little play for us. After which we will all have a Thanksgiving dinner together."

"That sounds like fun."

"Yes, I'm looking forward to seeing the youngsters in their homemade getups." Sophie sniffed her lavender sachet. "Maybe you could join us?"

"Maybe. I'll check the date against my schedule." Angela donned her coat, fished the car keys out of her purse, and leaned down to kiss Sophie's cheek. "I've got to go, I've a demographics study to work into a presentation before Wednesday. I'll see you next week."

"All right. Good night, dear."

"Good night." Angela blew her a kiss, closed the door, then sagged against it. Sophie and Leigh were relentless. She felt like a criminal with the posse closing in for the kill. Oh, if only she knew what to do.

Chapter Eleven

❧

Angela frowned and kept typing as the phone beside her rang. Thank heaven for answering machines or she'd never get done! The machine in the kitchen clicked on. She could hear Leigh's voice calling out her name, "Angela, pick up! Come on, Angela, *be* there, I need—"

She snatched up the receiver. "I'm here, Leigh, what's wrong? You sound—"

"Angela, I don't have time to talk. There's been a four-car pileup on the highway, and one of the women involved is seven months pregnant. I'm on my way in to try to save the baby. I need you to go see Hosea for me. Our meeting was set for eight o'clock tonight and I can't get him on the phone. I wouldn't ask, but this will be the third meeting Phil and I have had to cancel out on, and the time is getting short." There was a deep breath. "Angela you've got all the notes on the details of the wedding, would you please stand in for me?"

Angela's grip on the receiver tightened. "Oh, Leigh, I—"

"*Please*, Angela?" There was the thud of a car door closing. The sound of feet slapping against blacktop. "Hosea needs to know this stuff, so he can make his plans. Thanks Angela! Gotta turn off the phone now."

There was dead silence. Angela stared down at the receiver, then dropped it into its base and cradled her forehead in her hands. Why do these things keep happening? Two months. Two months she had avoided Hosea and now this!

She sighed and lifted her head to glance at the antique clock that graced the wall between the multipane windows at the far end of the room. Seven-forty-five. She had to leave now if she was going to make the scheduled meeting on time.

Reluctantly, she clicked the save button, pulled out her backup disk, found the notebook that contained the notes she had made on Leigh's wedding, and went to get her coat.

Hosea stared at the words on the monitor, shook his head in frustration and exited the program. He couldn't concentrate. He clasped his hands behind his neck, leaned back in his chair and stared up at the ceiling.

Angela was avoiding him again. And he knew she was hurting. He hated to see her hurting. He hated to see any of God's children hurting. But Angela's pain went so deep! As a pastor he knew God was working, and that the pain had to be brought to the surface where it could be skimmed off by the Savior's hand, that to interfere would only prolong the process. But, as a man, it was hard to keep from taking her in his arms and telling her it would be all right. He longed to protect—

The knock on his door broke into his thoughts. Hosea glanced at his watch, lunged to his feet and crossed the room to open the door.

"Well you two finally made it! I was beginning to think—" He stopped, staring in surprise at Angela. Pleasure coursed through him. The look of apprehension in her eyes brought him back to his senses. He reined in his emotions. "I'm sorry, Angela. I thought you were Leigh and Phil."

"I know." She tapped the notebook in her hands. "They're the reason I'm here."

"Oh?" Hosea looked down at the notebook. She was holding it against her chest like a shield. Against him? *Oh, God, help me to reach through her fear and touch her heart.* He pushed the door wide open and waved her into the room. "Am I to take your presence to mean there's been another emergency?"

"Yes, Phil had to fly to Denver—something to do with one of the buildings his company is erecting. And Leigh—well, there's been a four-car pileup on the highway and an injured woman in one of the vehicles is seven months pregnant. Leigh's trying to save the baby."

She glanced at his desk, then looked up at him. "Leigh couldn't get through on the phone, so she called and asked me to come in her stead." She nodded toward his telephone. "I guess that's the reason."

Hosea glanced at his phone. There was no receiver. "Well, how did—? Oh. I know." He frowned, and indicated a chair. "Have a seat, Angela. I'm sorry for your inconvenience."

He glanced around, then walked to another chair and lifted a plush pillow. "Ha! Gotcha!" He picked up the receiver lying underneath. "I loaned out my office to a couple for a private conversation earlier. I guess they didn't want to be interrupted."

The sound of the music team practicing Sunday's music filtered into the room through the open door as he dropped the receiver into place and turned to face her. "That's rough about the baby. Is the mother all right?"

Angela sat down and busied herself with her notebook. "I don't know. Leigh called me from her cell phone and she had to turn it off when she reached the hospital doors." Her hands stilled. "It must be serious though. I could hear her running from her car to the entrance."

Hosea nodded. "I'll remember them in my prayers." He lowered his hip to the corner of the desk, rested his forearm across his knee and joined his hands.

Angela stared at the few crisply curling blond hairs on their backs. What would it feel like if he touched her cheek?

"Was there something specific you wanted to discuss with me, Angela? Or did you come only to convey Leigh's regrets…again?"

Angela's errant thought collided with reality and came crashing to earth at the sound of Hosea's voice. What was wrong with her, thinking such foolish things? She tore her gaze away from his hands.

"If so—this will be the third time. She's a busy lady."

Angela lifted her head and their gazes met. Hosea's smile seemed to freeze in place. His hands clenched. He rose and moved to the other side of his desk.

Angela breathed a sigh of relief, then frowned and looked down at her hands. Had she been holding her breath? She gave herself a mental shake and made a concerted effort to gather her thoughts. "Actually, I'm here to do both. Leigh asked me to convey her apologies, and to be her stand-in to discuss the wedding plans with you, as time is growing short."

That was better. That sounded cool and business-like. She glanced up at him. "Is that acceptable?"

Hosea nodded. "Unusual…but perfectly acceptable." He dropped down into his chair.

Angela opened her notebook. "The first item Leigh mentioned is the unity candle." She glanced up as Hosea flipped open a tablet and picked up a pen. "Phil's parents are both gone, so no unity candle."

He drew a line through an item on a printed list and looked up at her. "Do they want to have their first communion together as man and wife during the ceremony?"

"Yes."

He made a check beside another item. "What about the vows?"

"They want the standard vows."

"All right." He made another check beside a third item and scratched a line through the fourth. "Any special music?"

"Yes." Angela consulted her notes. "While they

are having communion, they want 'May the Spirit of the Lord Descend Now on Me' played.'' She looked up. ''They want to say a joint prayer for their friends and family after they have communion. And, if you agree to that, during that time they want, 'You Are Never Alone' played in the background.'' She waited until Hosea stopped writing. ''After the prayer, they want Beverly Stoner to sing, 'One.'''

''Good choice! I agree completely.'' She watched as he jotted it down. ''Any more songs?''

''One more. If you approve, and agree with their wishes.'' She looked over her shoulder at a polite tap behind her.

Jeanne Barton smiled. ''Hi, Angela.'' She looked at Hosea. ''Pastor, sorry to interrupt, but Sandie wants to know if there will be time for a special anthem Sunday morning?''

Hosea nodded. ''A special will be great. We'll make time''

''Okay. Thanks.'' Jeanne stepped back into the hall and hurried away.

Hosea looked back at Angela. ''You were saying?''

She dropped her gaze to scan her notes and restore her train of thought that had been shattered by his smile. ''Based on the parable of the wise and foolish virgins in Matthew, chapter twenty-five, Leigh and Phil want to reverse the usual order of things.'' She glanced up. ''When it is time for the ceremony—that will be 7:00 p.m.—they want all the lights in the sanctuary dimmed. In the candlelight, Leigh will enter from the side door carrying an ancient-style oil lamp like the ones in Jerusalem. It will have a candle instead of oil in it for safety, of course.''

Hosea dropped his pen and leaned forward. Her heart thudded at the sudden, intense interest on his face. She looked back down. "She will walk to the altar, turn and face the center aisle. Then, Eric Spencer will sound his trumpet, the lights will come up, the double doors will open, and Phil will walk down the aisle to Leigh while Eric plays 'Perfect Love.' When the trumpet solo is over, the attendants will enter from the side doors and join them."

Hosea let out a soft whistle. "'And at midnight there was a cry made, Behold the bridegroom cometh.'" He leaned back in his chair and looked at her. "That's powerful."

Angela nodded. Her throat was too constricted to speak. For a long moment the silence held, then Hosea reached for his pen and jotted the information down.

"Anything else?"

Angela shook her head. "Only the decoration details, and I haven't worked them all out yet. But I do know we will want the large, self-standing candelabra. All six of them. Will they be available?"

"December fifteenth? Let me check." He pulled up a file on the computer. "Yes, they're available. I'll mark them for Leigh and Phil's use." He tapped a key, made a note on the list on his desk, then leaned back and rolled the pen between his palms. "You will be doing the decorations?"

"Yes."

"Then—judging from past performance—the sanctuary will be beautiful. Your decorations for the Missionary Conference were amazing.''

''Thank you. But Leigh—''

''Runs and fetches. She told me she's the mechanic...you're the decorator.''

Angela felt a warm flush creeping up her neck into her cheeks. She looked down and closed her notebook. ''Leigh is too modest.''

She rose to her feet and glanced across the desk as Hosea did likewise. ''I've taken enough of your time. Thank you for allowing me to stand in for Leigh. I know she appreciates it. She was concerned about missing another meeting with the wedding less than a month away.''

''Time is getting short.'' Hosea closed his notes. ''Will you be decorating the banquet room at The River House for the reception?''

Angela shook her head. ''I haven't the time or equipment. That room is huge! They have a professional group from Denver coming in to decorate it.''

Hosea let out a long, soft whistle.

Angela smiled in spite of her tension. ''That's what I said. But, as Leigh and Phil pointed out, they're only doing this once, so they might as well do it up big.''

Hosea grinned and moved around the desk to join her as she headed for the door. ''I'm not sure *big* covers this. *Tremendous* might come close.'' His fingers itched to touch her, to take her arm, to brush her cheek. He shoved his hands into his pockets and walked beside her down the wide hallway toward the entrance area.

''I've performed a lot of weddings, but never one

based on the Biblical precedent of the wise and foolish virgins. This will be one I'll never forget. And neither will anyone else that attends.'' Hosea lifted Angela's coat from the rack and held it out for her.

''I'm sure you're right.'' Angela slipped her arms into her coat and crossed to the double entrance doors. ''Thank you, again, for your time.''

''Before you go…'' Hosea yanked his hand out his pocket and grabbed hold of the push bar on the door. ''I've been wanting to ask if you've heard from Cathy. I'd like to know how she's doing.''

Angela smiled. The amber flecks in her brown eyes glowed. Hosea gripped the bar so tightly his fingers cramped.

''She's doing fine. I've been calling her once or twice a week to chat.'' She looked away. ''I want her to know someone cares about her. *Really* cares about her.''

She glanced down at his hand holding the door, then back up at him. ''She needs a computer. She's been doing her work on the ones the college makes available for students, but that means she has to wait, or do her work at odd hours. I'm working on earning another bonus, now. That's what I was doing when Leigh called.''

Her smile reached right out and snagged his heart. For a moment Hosea lost track of her words. Her frown brought him back to his senses.

''If I can work hard and fast enough to earn one more bonus before the holidays, I should have enough to get Cathy a computer for Christmas.''

''What a wonderful gift for her.'' Almost as wonderful as you are for wanting to give it, he thought. Hosea swallowed back the words he wanted so much to say and smiled. "That being the case, I guess I'd better not take up any more of your time talking. But, if the holidays catch you before you have earned enough, let me know. I'd be delighted to help. Maybe the church could provide the printer and a scanner? If you wouldn't mind, of course."

Hosea's heart sank at the tears that swam into Angela's eyes. "What is it? Did I say something wrong?"

She shook her head and blinked away the tears. "No. Nothing. What you suggest would be wonderful. Cathy would know the whole church family cares about her." Her voice broke. She turned toward the door.

"Angela?"

She pushed against the door. "I have to go. Good night, Pastor."

Reluctantly, Hosea released his grip and let the door open. "Good night, Angela. I'll see you Sunday morning."

She nodded and rushed outside.

In spite of the frosty air, Hosea stepped outdoors to watch her go. *Lord, she's so beautiful. Inside and out, You've made her so beautiful.*

He felt suddenly lonely, bereft, as she drove away. When her car disappeared from sight it was as if his heart departed with her. For a long moment he stood staring at the empty road, then he turned and went inside.

How long, Lord? How long do I have to wait until I can make Angela mine?

Chapter Twelve

"Aren't they cute?"

Angela smiled and nodded. "Very cute. But not too accurate."

Sophie chuckled. "That's true. That boy looks more like a swashbuckling pirate than a pilgrim. And look at the fourth pumpkin. I've never seen a furry pumpkin before. But the green stem hat is quite the thing."

"It certainly is." Angela's gaze fastened on the wide blue eyes, round pink cheeks, and pointed little chin surrounded by stiff, green-striped fabric. "And the little girl wearing it is adorable." She couldn't quite keep the longing out of her voice.

Sophie shot her a quick look. "You know, I wouldn't mind having an 'adopted' greatgrand-daughter."

Angela stiffened.

"Speaking of which—have you made up with Hosea yet?"

"Sophie..."

A swish of Sophie's aged, thin-skinned hand brushed away the warning. "Well, have you? I know it's not really any of my business, but you're not getting any younger. And, more to the point, neither am I."

Angela laughed. She couldn't help it. Sophie was adorable herself. But, just the same, the laughter was all too close to tears. She took a breath and shook her head. "I'm not going to discuss Hosea Stevens with you, Sophie. I came to Pine Glen to watch a parade."

"Of other people's children!"

"Yes, Sophie, of other people's children." The words cut deep into the wounded place in her heart. Angela fought down the pain and fixed a smile on her face. Sophie didn't mean to hurt her. She didn't know it would always be other people's children for her.

"I don't want to. I don't *want* to be Priscilla!"

Angela turned around. There was a costumed child in the archway. A teacher drew the little girl back out of the open arch and squatted down in front of her. It was Marilyn Harris. Angela could hear her church friend's low voice reasoning with the child.

"Now, Joanie…remember how we talked about how much fun it would be to show all these nice people what happened when our country celebrated the first Thanksgiving?"

The little girl nodded. "I wanted to then—I don't want to now." She tugged at the bow under her chin and the ties fell free.

"I understand, Joanie, but—"

"Mrs. Harris, my feathers fell down."

Angela smiled. A little boy with construction paper feathers hanging in front of his eyes was tugging at Marilyn's sleeve.

"You'll have to wait a minute, Lenny."

"But, Mrs. Harris, I have to go up and say my lines next!"

"Oh, that's right." Marilyn Harris pulled a roll of tape from her pocket. "Joanie, you have to say your part in just a moment. Please tie your bonnet in place while I fix Lenny's feathers." She ripped a piece of tape from the roll and squatted down to deal with the torn, lopsided native headdress.

"I don't *want* to!" The little girl set her jaw and crossed her arms.

Angela touched Sophie's thin shoulder. "I'll be back shortly, Sophie. I think Marilyn could use some help." She stepped around the end of the row of chairs, walked through the archway and smiled down at the pouting little girl.

"Hi Joanie, I'm Angela. And I think that is just the cutest dress and bonnet. But your ties are undone. May I fix them for you?" She knelt down and began to tie them in a bow under the child's chin before she could refuse.

Marilyn Harris twisted her head to look over her shoulder. Her eyes lit with recognition and her lips curved in a smile of gratitude.

Angela smiled back, and pulled the ends of the bow even. "There. Oh, my, that looks pretty." She leaned back and whistled softly. "I'll bet John Alden and Miles Standish won't even *look at* Priscilla again when they see you in that bonnet."

The little girl giggled. "I'm Priscilla."

"You are?"

The brim of the bonnet bobbed as the little girl nodded in acknowledgment.

"Then you'd better hurry up front. I think I just heard John Alden call your name." Angela turned the child around toward the archway and gave her a gentle, encouraging nudge. The little girl stood there for a moment, then smiled at Angela and yelled, "I'm coming, John Alden!" Hiking her long skirts up above her dimpled knees she ran to the front of the large room.

"Thanks for stepping in, Angela." Marilyn Harris threw her a grateful look. "My aide called in sick at the last minute and I'm a little overwhelmed." She ripped off another piece of tape, secured the last feather in Lenny's headband, then turned toward the milling children and clapped her hands softly. "Turkeys, line up over here please."

A small girl pushed forward and tugged at the teacher's skirt. "Mrs. Harris? I have to go to the bathroom."

"Oh, Ingrid, can't you wait?" Marilyn shot a desperate glance into the other room where there was a sudden dead silence. "I have to go help Miles Standish—he's forgotten his lines."

"I'll take her."

"Would you?" Marilyn Harris spun toward Angela. She nodded. "I'll be happy to."

"You're an angel! Thank you." The teacher put her hand on the little girl's shoulder. "Ingrid, go with Miss Warren—and hurry back. The turkeys are on next.'' She lifted her finger to her lips. ''Shhhh, everyone. Not a gobble while you wait for my signal to come onstage.'' She pivoted about and hurried to Miles Standish's rescue.

Angela stretched out her hand toward the child. ''Hi, Ingrid. Come with me. I'll show you where the bathroom is.''

The little girl stared up at her. ''You're pretty. Are you in the play?''

Angela shook her head. ''No, I'm not, but it looks like fun.''

''Well, do you know how to get my feathers off so I can go potty?''

''I think I can figure it out.''

''Okay, then. But we have to hurry.'' Ingrid thrust her small hand into Angela's.

Angela's chest tightened. She smiled down at the little girl. ''I'll tell you what—we'll go as fast as if we were both real turkeys with wings.''

''So how was the Thanksgiving parade?'' Leigh reached for a cookie and took a bite. ''Yum! These are good. What are they?''

''Farmer's cookies.'' Angela laid one on her plate. ''The parade and play were very nice. Colorful and…spontaneous.''

Leigh grinned. ''I know what you mean. Little kids are a hoot, aren't they? They're so honest and direct about everything. And cute enough to get away with it.''

''That's certainly true.'' Angela rose and walked to the stove for the tea kettle.

"How's Sophie?"

Angela smiled and filled their mugs with the boiling water. "She's fine. She had a wonderful time chatting with the children over dinner."

"Hmm, I'll bet." Leigh added sugar to her tea and stirred. "From what you've told me, she's almost as plainspoken as the children."

"That's for sure." Sophie's remark about other people's children snapped into Angela's mind. Tears stung the backs of her eyes. She turned back to put the teapot on the stove.

"What's wrong, Angela?"

The tears flowed into her eyes at Leigh's concerned tone. She blinked them away and returned to the table. "You're asking that an awful lot lately."

"That's because you always avoid answering me."

Angela forced a grin. "Then I guess the smart thing would be to give up." She broke off a piece of cookie and laid it down.

"Take a bite, Angela."

"What?"

Leigh inclined her head toward Angela's plate. "You're not fooling me by breaking your food apart, or pushing it around on your plate." Her gaze lifted to fasten on Angela's overly bright eyes. "I want to see you actually take a bite of food, chew and swallow it."

"Don't be silly." Angela pushed back from the table, but Leigh's hand snagged her wrist before she could rise.

"I'm not being silly. I'm dead serious, Angela. If

you don't start eating you're going to make yourself sick. Your body needs fuel.''

Angela cringed as Leigh's gaze scanned her face.

''Why won't you tell me what's wrong? Are you ill? Is that why you're unable to eat or sleep? If so, I can help. I know specialists—''

''I'm not ill!'' Angela jerked her hand away. ''I just have a…a problem. And I told you before I'm not going to discuss it. Now, I'll get my notebook and we can go over the wedding decorations. I have a new idea for the railing I think you'll like.''

She jumped up from the table, opened the drawer in the hutch and brought back a sketchbook. ''Here it is. Now see, I think these bouquets on the newel posts will be better. The floral roping was too much in my opinion. What do you think?'' Her eyes begged Leigh to pretend everything was all right.

Leigh sighed and looked down at the drawing. ''I like them. Of course I liked the floral roping for the railing, too, so I guess I'm not much of a judge.''

''Oh, Leigh, you're always selling yourself short. You need to stop that. You have wonderful taste.'' Angela flipped the page to another drawing. ''Now, this is what I was thinking of for the communion table….''

''Hi, Leigh. Come on in.'' Hosea pushed the door wide, helped Leigh off with her coat and waved her to a chair. ''Now, what's this emergency meeting about? Last-minute wedding panic?''

He draped her coat over a chair and turned to face

her. She was still standing. His smile faded at the look on her face. "What's wrong?"

"I don't know. I thought maybe you could tell me."

He studied her face for a moment, then started for his desk chair. "You'll have to give me a clue."

The click of the door closing stopped him dead in his tracks. He turned around.

Leigh moved forward. "I want the door closed, Pastor. I don't want this conversation overheard. Phil is standing guard in the hall so we won't be interrupted."

Pastor, not Hosea. Phil on guard? Hosea nodded. "All right. What's this about?"

"Angela."

Hosea's heart lurched. He turned and walked around behind his desk. "What about her?"

"I told you, I don't know. I only know something is terribly wrong." Leigh stepped closer, lowered her voice. "I don't know what it is, or how to help her. She won't talk to me about it. All she says is, she has a problem and she won't discuss it with me—now or ever."

Hosea remained quiet.

Leigh put her hands on his desk and leaned forward. "I also know it has something to do with you."

Hosea looked down into those green doctor's eyes of hers and knew there was no use denying it. "Only indirectly, Leigh."

She stared at him. "So you know what her problem is?"

"I believe so. Yes."

"Well, thank the Lord for that!" Leigh drew a deep

breath and blinked sudden moisture from her eyes as she straightened. "Can you tell me?"

He shook his head.

"But you *can* help her?"

Hosea weighed his words. "I believe I can. But not yet. I hope soon."

"What does that mean?"

"It means the Lord is working in Angela's heart. And sometimes—when the Lord is doing His work— even a pastor must keep his hands off that specific area until the time is right."

Leigh's eyes shimmered with tears. "So we simply sit back and watch her hurting, and do nothing?"

"No. Of course not." Hosea locked his gaze on Leigh's. "We continue to let her know that we love and care about her. And we minister to her in every way possible without intruding into that one area, or pushing her to tell us about it before she is ready."

He grabbed a handful of tissues from his desk drawer and handed them to her. "I know it's hard, Leigh. Especially for someone trained to gather all the pertinent facts, make a diagnosis and then do something to fix whatever is wrong. But it just doesn't always work that way in the spirit. Sometimes, if we force the issue, we ruin what the Lord is doing. And that makes everything worse."

He stepped around his desk and laid a comforting hand on her shoulder. "Trust the Lord, Leigh. Trust Him to do what is best for Angela."

Chapter Thirteen

"**W**ell, that's it folks. I'll see you back here to-morrow night at six o'clock for the real thing. And don't forget about the rehearsal dinner at Romans!"

By sheer dint of will, Hosea kept his gaze from seeking out Angela—kept his feet from walking to her side. Instead, he stepped down from the platform and walked over to where Judy Anderson sat a little apart from the chattering knot of people donning their coats and gathering up their possessions.

"How about a little help, Judy? It looks as if you could use another pair of hands."

"Oh, thank you, Pastor. Tom's home with the flu and it's a little hard to manage everything without him." She threw Hosea a grateful smile over top of the squirming baby on her lap. "This little guy does not like to get his snowsuit on. And the twins can't quite manage all the snaps, zippers and ties."

"I can zipper!"

"You can?" Hosea crouched down in front of the

three-year-old boy who was struggling to find his jacket's sleeve hole for his left arm. "Here you go." He held the jacket in place, then pulled it snugly about the boy's small body. "Now, let's see you zipper."

The toddler gave him a look of pure exasperation. "You gots to start it first."

"Oh. I'm sorry. I didn't know." Hosea fought back a grin and slid the two ends of the zipper together. "I don't have any little boys so I'm not quite sure how this goes."

The toddler stared at him a moment, then nodded acceptance of that explanation as he gripped the zipper tab in his pudgy little hand and tugged it upward. "You gonna get some boys?"

"Peter!"

Hosea laughed. He glanced up at the embarrassed mother. "It's all right, Judy. It's a perfectly logical question." He looked back at the little boy who was tugging his knitted hat in place. "Not right now, Peter—but I hope to someday."

There was a small tug on his sleeve. Hosea turned his head and looked into a pair of round hazel eyes in a pixie face framed by russet curls held prisoner by elastic bands with large blue beads on them.

"Will you get some girls, too? I could play wif them."

Hosea pulled the toddler close. "I sure hope so, Penny. Especially if they're as bright and pretty as you." Her delighted smile filled his chest with longing. He pushed the emotion away. It would happen—in God's time.

He circled Peter with his other arm. "You two did

a really good job, tonight. And I know tomorrow evening you'll do even better.''

Penny's russet curls bobbed as she nodded agreement. She leaned back and held her jacket out to Hosea. "I pretend flowers good. Mommy said so."

"You certainly do. Mommy's absolutely right." Hosea zipped her into her jacket, then reached into the pocket, extracted a pair of mittens and pulled them on over her little hands. "But tomorrow night you won't have to pretend—you'll have real flower petals to scatter."

The little girl giggled. "*Scatter* is a funny word."

"So's *pigtail*." Hosea gave one of hers a gentle tug, then pulled her hood up and tied it under her chin as she and her twin brother dissolved in laughter.

"Angela? Do you want a ride to the rehearsal dinner?"

Angela started and tore her gaze away from Hosea and the children to look up at Phil's brother. "I'm sorry, I didn't hear you."

He jingled his car keys in the space between them.

"Oh." She smiled and shook her head. "Thanks anyway, Bob. But I have my car."

"Okay." He zipped his jacket closed. "Just thought I'd offer. Best man stuff, you know. I'm taking my wedding responsibilities seriously."

"I'm glad to hear it, because Phil's a wreck."

A grin spread across Bob's face. "Yeah...he's pretty nervous all right. He's worried Leigh will be called away from the ceremony to perform some emergency surgery or something.'' He laughed and lifted a hand in farewell. ''See you at the restaurant.''

''Yes.'' A sudden explosion of laughter from Hosea and the Anderson twins made Angela turn. Pain stabbed into her heart. He was bouncing them, one on each broad shoulder, as he jogged toward the door. She looked away, but it was too late, the image was already burned into her mind.

Angela clenched her hands and hurried toward the women's rest room before the ache in her heart got worse—before it burst out in a wave of anger, bitterness and sorrow that would help nothing. She rushed into a stall, closed the door, then sagged back against it.

Why? Why? Why?

Angela closed her eyes and tried to breathe through the pain. Why did Hosea's presence bring such agonizing awareness of just how much the lifestyle her mother and stepfather had forced her into was going to cost her? Why did she have to learn, now—when it was too late—that there were decent, honorable men who loved, cared for and protected children? Men who would love and be faithful to the woman who loved them. Men like Hosea.

Hosea.

Oh, why did she have to meet Hosea?

A sob burst from her throat. Angela lifted her hands to cover her mouth and spun about to hide her face against the stall door. What did God want from her? She had already forgiven her parents and Tony. And she had begged countless times for forgiveness herself. What was God after?

Do you know your God? The words Hosea had spoken in last Sunday's sermon flowed into Angela's mind. *We say we know our God. And we believe it with all our hearts. But the moment we have a problem—the moment we find ourselves in unpleasant, or painful situations—we think, What is God after? What does He want from me? Well, the answer could be...nothing. It could be He wants to bless you.*

If you truly know your God, then you will know He's not some gigantic authority in the sky just waiting for an opportunity to snatch away our health, happiness, or prosperity. He's our Father. He loves us. And He uses the muddy morass of the difficult circumstances we humans create for ourselves and others as an opportunity to work for our good. Remember what it says in Romans, chapter eight, verse twenty-eight? "And we know that in all things God works for the good of those who love Him, who have been called according to His purpose."

Angela took a deep breath and brushed the tears from her cheeks. She believed in God's word—and she loved Him with her whole heart. But, what good could God possibly work out of her situation? She was an ex-prostitute in love with a pastor. The best she could hope for was that God would help her live with the pain of knowing there was no future for them.

Despair gripped her anew. Angela went to the sink to splash cold water on her burning eyes. She had to get through the rehearsal dinner tonight, and the wedding and reception tomorrow evening—she had given Leigh her word.

The thought of the wedding almost did her in. Drawing on her old trick, Angela made her mind an absolute blank and walked out to get her coat and join the others headed for their cars.

Chapter Fourteen

The wind howled around the corner of the building, swirling the falling snow into a blinding curtain of white. Angela braked, then crept forward into the parking space closest to the doors and shut off the motor.

She pulled the notched collar of her long, caramel-colored wool coat up around her neck, and climbed out into the storm. The cold stole her breath away. Her eyes watered. Tiny ice crystals formed on her eyelashes.

She lifted her gloved hands to cover her nose and mouth, and hurried around the car to the trunk and raised the lid. Box after box of decorations filled the space. Thank goodness Leigh had decided on silk flowers. Fresh flowers would be frozen before she could get them unloaded. In this weather *she* could be frozen before she got them all unloaded.

Angela stomped her feet—which were already going numb from the cold—stacked two small boxes on top of a large one, balanced the pile in one arm and slammed the trunk lid down to protect the others.

The snow squeaked under her feet as she ducked her head into her collar and hurried in the direction of the doors. Between the boxes and the snow she couldn't see a thing. Hopefully, she wouldn't maim herself on the stairs. Not a happy thought.

Angela slowed her pace and stuck her head out to peek around the boxes, getting a stinging face full of snow for the effort. She blinked to clear her eyes, took another step forward and promptly went reeling backward as she ran smack-dab into something. Her feet slid. The boxes teetered.

"Ohhh!"

Strong hands grabbed her arms—steadied her. Angela couldn't see who her benefactor was because of her streaming eyes, but her heart knew. She didn't resist when the packages were taken from her. She just hid her head behind Hosea's broad, snow-covered shoulders and followed him inside.

She almost rammed into him again when he stopped abruptly and turned around.

"Where's Mike Eldridge? I thought he was supposed to bring these things to the church for you."

The question caught her totally off guard—as did the tone of voice. Angela stopped stomping the snow from her boots and looked up at Hosea. "Mike caught that bug that's going around. He's home in bed nursing a fever." She stared at the muscle that ran along Hosea's square jaw. It was twitching. Was he angry with Mike?

"Why didn't you call me to help, Angela? You

shouldn't be lifting these large boxes. And with the roads as bad as they are, I would have come after you in the church's SUV. A four-wheel-drive vehicle is a lot safer in weather like this.''

Her breath caught. Angela lifted her gaze to Hosea's eyes. He wasn't angry with Mike, he was worried…about *her*. Warmth settled around her heart and spread outward, driving away the cold. ''I'm sorry. I didn't think to call. I'm used to taking care of myself. I've never had anyone to help me.''

''You do now.''

The words were spoken so quietly she almost missed them. Her pulse quickened.

''Where do you want these things?''

''I— On the platform in the sanctuary.''

Hosea nodded and headed that direction. She turned back toward the door.

''Where are you going?''

Angela whipped around. He had stopped by the sanctuary doors. ''I'm going to the car. There are more boxes to be brought in.''

''I'll get them. It's icy out there. You might fall.''

''But you have work—'' The look that sprang into Hosea's eyes closed Angela's throat, choking off her protest.

''I've nothing more important to do.''

The sudden, soft warmth in Hosea's voice turned Angela's legs to jelly. She groped for the coatrack. Hangers clattered to the floor. She stared down at them. What could she do? She couldn't allow this to happen! She drew a deep breath. ''All right, Pastor Stevens. Thank you. It is bitter out there.''

She heard the quick intake of Hosea's breath at her deliberate use of his formal title. Was it caused by anger—or hurt?

Tears pricked Angela's eyes. She didn't want to hurt him. She bent forward and picked up a hanger. Reached for another. She could feel him staring at her.

Her mouth went dry at the sound of movement. Without lifting her head, she darted her gaze toward Hosea. He'd put the boxes down! He took a step toward her. Took another. Stopped. Her heart thudded. His hands clenched, opened. Abruptly, he turned, picked up the boxes and shoved through the swinging doors into the sanctuary.

Angela dropped the hangers, pushed to her feet and ran toward the women's bathroom. She had to hide until he was gone.

Hide. Angela shoved through the bathroom door and clenched her hands into fists to keep from slamming the doors on every stall. Her breath came in short gasps. That's what she'd done all her life—hide. She'd hidden from her mother and stepfather. Hidden from the men they'd traded her to for drugs or money. Hidden from fear and terror, filth and decadence...and evil. And now—now she was hiding from decency, honor, goodness and love!

She turned and stared out the window, hugging herself against the anger that shook her body, biting her lower lip to keep from screaming at the injustice of it all. None of that would change anything. The futility of her situation washed over her. She took a deep breath, then took another. The anger abated. But not the pain. She closed her eyes and began to pray. She needed strength from the Lord to enable her to do her decorating in the sanctuary when Hosea left.

> "'I will praise You, Lord, in the early morning hours.
> I will praise You, Lord, throughout the day.
> And when, at night, the stars come out to shine;
> I will praise You from the bed on which I lay....'"

Angela sang softly as she worked. She'd been singing all morning, concentrating on the words of the songs to keep her own thoughts at bay. She lifted her voice into the chorus.

> "'For You are wor-r-thy, You are wor-r-thy.
> You, alone, Lord, are worthy of my praise.
> Holy Lord, above, looking down on me with love.
> You, alone are worthy of my praise.'"

She tucked more baby's breath in one of the candelabra arrangements and added the bow. Now for the candles.

"Time for lunch."

Angela spun around. Hosea's head was stuck through an opening in the double doors. "I don't have time—"

His head disappeared. A moment later the door opened and he started down the center aisle carrying a pizza box. There was a baby blanket from the nursery draped over his arm. "I thought you'd say that, Angela. But I'm trusting your good manners won't let you refuse to eat what I've already paid for."

He didn't even look at her. He just stepped through the open door to the small multipurpose room off the platform, spread the blanket on the floor, set the box in the center and pulled two bottles of water from his pockets. She didn't know what to do.

"Let's see…green peppers, black olives and mushrooms. No onions—because of the wedding tonight—and no pepperoni." He glanced up at her. "Did I get it right?"

He'd remembered! From months ago. Angela couldn't speak. She nodded. While she watched, he produced paper napkins and two oranges from another pocket, laid them on the blanket, then stepped to the edge of the platform and smiled up at her. "Your lunch awaits you, madam." He made a sweeping movement with his arm toward the blanket.

She had no choice. Angela took a deep breath, laid the candles she was holding on the table and walked down to join him.

The potent smell of pizza filled the small room when Hosea opened the box. He chuckled, tore off a piece, placed it on a napkin and held it out to her. "I didn't think about the smell. We'll have to get rid of it somehow, or Leigh will bolt from the altar and head for the nearest pizza place."

The sight of Hosea, dressed in his suit and tie, sitting cross-legged on a baby blanket on the floor so he could bring her lunch, all but destroyed the tight rein

Angela held on her emotions. She forced a smile and took the pizza. "I have potpourri."

Hosea took a piece of pizza for himself. "I hope it's strong. If not, there's probably some pretty overwhelming squirt stuff in the janitor's closet." He took a bite of his pizza. "Hmm, this is good."

Angela nodded and took a bite out of her piece. Hosea smiled at her. Her throat closed. He had such a beautiful smile. She lowered her lashes and looked out from under them, feasting on the sight of him while he ate pizza.

"The decorations are beautiful, Angela. I've never seen any draping over a railing like that." He fastened his gaze on her. "You're very talented."

"Thank you." She didn't dare meet his gaze—her emotions were too near the surface. It was getting harder and harder to hide them. She dipped her head and took another bite of pizza. She'd eat it if she choked!

"My mom and my sister Hannah would give their eye teeth to be able to make decorations like these." Hosea popped the last of his piece into his mouth and chuckled. "I'm afraid it would take a miracle to pull it off, though. I've seen their attempts at decorating."

"I didn't know you had a sister." Angela stared at her pizza. She might as well be eating cardboard. She took another bite.

"Yep. She's three years older than me." Hosea took a long drink of water, then broke off another piece of pizza. The hot, melted cheese stretched out into a long, thin string, then broke. He piled it on top of his piece, licked the sauce from his fingers and wiped them dry on his napkin. "She made my life miserable when I was small. She mothered me to death." He grinned a lopsided grin that made Angela's insides go all jittery. "Then I grew bigger than her. That stopped the mothering. We're great friends now. I miss her."

"Miss her?" She'd never get this bite swallowed. Angela reached for her water and forced the pizza down.

Hosea nodded. "She's married to a career Marine. Right now, they're in Germany. Mom and Dad miss her so much. And now I'm out here." He wiped his mouth and took a swallow of water. "They know it's the Lord's will for me, and they're happy about that. But it's still pretty hard on them having both kids so far away. They'd really be lonely if they didn't have their church family."

"They sound nice." What would it be like to have parents that loved you? Angela wondered. Her throat constricted around a piece of crust. She reached for the water again.

"They are. I'd love them even if they weren't my parents. All the kids in our neighborhood do. A lot of young people have come to the Lord because of my parents."

"Is your father a pastor, too?"

Hosea shook his head. Light glinted off his blond hair. Angela looked away and put the last bite of her pizza in her mouth.

"I'm the first pastor in our family. My dad's a carpenter. Not just houses. He makes furniture, too. He can do anything. And my mother's a mom.'' He grinned. ''That's capital M-O-M. She's terrific.''

The love and pride on Hosea's face as he talked about his mother and father made Angela ache with longing. She choked down the last bite and wiped her mouth.

''Ready for another?''

She shook her head. Hosea reached for an orange. Thank heaven he was finished, too. She couldn't take much more.

''How's Cathy doing? I haven't talked to her this week.''

Relief surged through Angela at the safe topic. ''She's doing fine. She's sure she's done well on all her tests.'' She glanced up at his face, then quickly realized that was a mistake and looked back down to watch him peel his orange. She loved his hands. She loved everything about him. Her eyes filled. She ducked her head and blinked the tears away.

''Thank you for lunch, Hosea, but I have to get back to work or I'll never finish on time.'' She pushed to her feet, and reached for her water bottle and crumpled napkin.

Hosea stayed her hand. ''I'll clear this stuff out of your way, Angela. I know you're busy.'' He released her hand and rose to stand beside her. ''It all just goes in the trash, anyway.''

''All right.'' She could still feel his hand on hers. She stared down at her tingling flesh and started for the platform.

''Angela?''

''Yes?''

"You forgot your orange."

She turned and looked at the orange he held out to her. It was the peeled one. He had peeled the orange for her. The tenderness of the gesture was her undoing.

The last of Angela's strength to resist Hosea crumbled. She felt it falling away, leaving her open, vulnerable, without protection. She reached for the orange. "Thank you. Thank you, Hosea, for…for everything."

She closed her eyes against the soft, betraying whisper. She hadn't meant it to come out like that.

"You're welcome, Angela…for everything."

His voice was soft, deep, intimate. She couldn't breathe. She waited for him to turn away, but he stayed. She could hear him breathing, could feel his gaze on her face. Tears burned behind her closed eyes. She wanted so much to step into Hosea's arms—to feel their strength holding her, protecting her, loving her. She wanted so much to love him in return. But if he knew the truth he would only push her away. *Oh, God, help me turn away. I have to have strength to turn away. For him, Lord. For him.*

Tears spilled from her eyes and splashed onto the orange she held clutched to her heart as she climbed the steps and walked over to pick up the candles she had laid on the table.

She was finished. This was the last one. Angela made a small adjustment to the string of pearls she had twined in and out among the ivory satin and ecru lace ribbons of the bow in her hands. She attached it to the end of the pew beside her and stepped back to sweep her gaze down the long aisle.

Everything was in place. Every ribbon, flower and pearl arranged as perfectly as her ability allowed.

She walked forward slowly, checking the positions of each flower and ribbon in the arrangements on the six candelabra of varying heights standing on the platform—making certain every taper was perfectly straight. One last time she scanned the floral arrangement on the communion table, the crystal goblets and decanter of grape juice, the covered bread and linen napkins.

She shifted her gaze to the other side of the table and checked the silver lighter and candle snuffer. All was as it should be. She had done the best she could for her friend. Now there was the wedding and reception to get through.

Angela lifted the box of boutonnieres from the front pew and carried it to the women's changing room where it would be safe. Her breath caught at sight of the beautiful wedding gown hanging in its clear plastic bag on the opposite wall.

She turned her back on the gown and hurried to the table along the side wall to place the box beside the bouquets she had made for Leigh and her attendants to carry. Her own maid of honor bouquet laid among them. The smarting behind her eyes increased. She ran from the room, slamming the door behind her.

If only she could close out her thoughts as easily. All day long she had tried to make her mind a blank, to distance herself from her emotions as she used to do. It wasn't working.

Painful pressure filled Angela's chest as she hurried back to the sanctuary. She would have to pin a boutonniere on Hosea tonight. She closed her eyes and took a deep breath. ''Oh, Lord, help me. My hands are trembling at the mere thought of being so close to him.''

Angela wrenched her eyes open and glanced down at her watch—three o'clock—and she had to be back here by six. It would be close, but she could make it if she hurried. Thank heaven the snow had stopped. Hosea had come in a few minutes ago to report the roads had been cleared. He'd been eating an orange.

Angela shook her head. She didn't want to think about oranges. She gave a last quick glance around to be sure she hadn't overlooked anything, then grabbed her box of tape, florist wire and tools, and hurried from the sanctuary.

The tears she'd been holding back all day started the moment she closed her front door. She couldn't restrain them. Angela put down the box, started up the stairs, then sank down onto a step and buried her face in her hands.

I'm in love with him. Oh, God, I'm in love with him! There was such pressure in her chest she couldn't breathe. She gasped for air and pressed her fingertips against her eyelids to stem the tears. They just ran down her arms, soaking into her sleeves.

How did this happen? Oh, God, how did this happen? I hate men! I don't trust them! And now I love him. I love him! Angela wrapped her arms about herself and rocked to-and-fro.

Why did You let me fall in love with him, Lord? Of all the men in the world, why did You let me fall in love with him? Why? Is this my punishment for my sin of prostitution? Is that what all this is, Lord, my punishment? Weren't the years of terror enough? Must I endure this pain, too?

There was no answer. But why would there be? She deserved this. She deserved it all. But not Hosea. No, never Hosea. She couldn't smear him with her sin. Slowly Angela rose to her feet and started up the stairs again. She had to get ready for the wedding.

Chapter Fifteen

"**Y**ou're trembling."

Angela closed out the warmth in Hosea's voice and concentrated on the boutonniere in her hand. It was shaking so hard there would be nothing left but a stem by the time she got it pinned to his lapel. *Lord, help me. I have to do this.*

"What is it about a wedding that makes women so nervous?"

He was trying to help her. He was so thoughtful. So kind. So heart-stoppingly handsome! Angela tugged her mind away from that thought and slid her hand under Hosea's lapel. "I can't speak for the others, but this is my first wedding."

She held her breath, put the boutonniere in place and raised the pearl florist's pin.

"Well, if I have my way, it's not going to be your last."

Angela's hand jerked—the end of the pin buried itself in her finger. She closed her eyes, stuck the end of her finger in her mouth and bit down hard to get control. He couldn't have meant— He was only talking about the decorations. Get hold of yourself!

"Angela, I'm sorry. I shouldn't have said—"

"Pastor?"

Hosea pivoted.

"Phil sent me to find you. He needs to see you right away." Bob stepped closer and bent down to pick up the boutonniere that had fallen to the floor. "Sharp pin, Angela?"

She nodded and reached for the flower.

Hosea took it from Bob's hand. "I'll put this on, Angela." His voice softened. "Maybe you'd better go run some cold water on your finger. You wouldn't want to get blood on Leigh's gown."

"Why? She'd feel right at home, Pastor." Bob grinned at them both. "Leigh's used to the sight of blood."

"So she is." Hosea finished pinning the flower in place. "Did I get it straight?"

Angela forced a smile and nodded. "It's perfect."

Hosea locked his gaze on hers. "Yes it is. Just perfect."

"Well, okay then—the problem of the boutonniere is settled." Bob clapped Hosea on the shoulder. "Let's go, Pastor. My brother is one nervous groom."

Hosea nodded. "All right, Bob. Let's go see if we can calm him down."

Angela stood rooted to the floor, watching Hosea as he walked away.

"And do you, Leigh Anne Roberts, take this man..."

Angela swallowed hard and blinked her eyes. She

could do this. She could get through this wedding for her friend's sake. But, oh how much easier it would be if she could just tune out the sound of Hosea's voice—if she wasn't so conscious of him standing only a few feet from her.

Angela looked down at the bouquet in her hand, then lifted her gaze to the candelabra and closely studied the cascading arrangements of flowers, ribbon and lace that tumbled from beneath the flaming candles to the floor.

She should have added a tiny bit more baby's breath in that spot on the right. She shifted her gaze to the communion table. Someone had put the silver candle lighter down in the wrong place, and—

"Ladies and gentlemen—may I present Mr. and Mrs. Philip Johnson!"

The sanctuary erupted into a burst of applause.

Angela started. It was over. She had made it through the wedding. Breathing a sigh of relief, she moved forward to adjust Leigh's train. Now if she could just get through the reception.

She straightened, slipped her hand through Bob's offered arm and walked beside him up the aisle at the prescribed distance behind the bride and groom. The rest of the wedding party fell into line behind them.

Angela blinked and swallowed. Thank heaven tears were commonplace at weddings—she couldn't keep them from her eyes. She curved her lips into a smile as cameras flashed, then took a deep breath, hugged and kissed Phil and Leigh, wished them God's richest blessings and stepped to her place in the receiving line.

Bob glanced back toward the sanctuary. "Looks like this is going to take some time. I think the entire population of Harmony is here, not to mention out-of-town friends and relatives. We may not eat before midnight."

Angela brushed away the tears pooling at the corners of her eyes and smiled at the whispered aside. "Are you hungry, Bob?"

Phil's brother grinned down at her. "I could eat a bear and have room for a buffalo! But I'll happily settle for the chicken or whatever they're serving at the reception."

"Bobby! You make such a handsome 'Best Man.'"

Angela fought back laughter at the pained look on Bob's face as his childhood name was called out. She was afraid to laugh. Afraid it would turn into a crying jag she couldn't control.

"Hello, Aunt Ruth. It's nice to see you."

A large, gray-haired woman enveloped Bob in a crushing hug. He extricated himself and gestured toward Angela. "May I introduce you to Leigh's best friend—Angela Warren. Angela, my aunt, Ruth Barrett."

Angela submitted herself to a warm, somewhat stifling hug, and the rest was a blur of names, faces and flashing camera lights.

"Doesn't Leigh look beautiful, Angela?"

"Yes she does, Emily."

"The whole wedding was beautiful. You did a wonderful job on the decorations, Angela. You're so talented!"

"Thank you."

"Yes, it's lovely that you girls are able to trade services. Perhaps Mrs. Johnson will return the favor when you marry."

Angela stiffened at the condescending tone in Ina Fleming's voice and the speculative gleam in the older woman's eyes. For all her pretentious ways, she was the worst, most malicious, gossip in the church. "I doubt that, Mrs. Fleming. Leigh's job keeps her much too busy. And with a new husband…" She let her voice trail off and looked across the table.

"You're so right, Angela." Iris Benton took the bait and jumped into the conversation. "There are a lot of adjustments to be made in a new marriage. And when children come along—"

"Oh my, yes!" Courtney Lewis grinned and shook her head. "I remember when Zachary was born…."

They were off and running. Angela wiggled her fingers in farewell at the small cluster of women and headed for the door. She had to get away for a few moments. Her head ached, and her face was sore from forcing smiles all evening. But most of all, she was exhausted from avoiding Hosea. If only she could go home.

"Angela?"

Oh, no. Angela looked wistfully at the door, then turned and smiled as Patty Miller and a handful of young, single women from the church came bearing down on her.

"Hello, Patty. What can I do for you?"

"We came to get you. Leigh's about to throw her bouquet!"

Angela's stomach knotted. She forced another smile as the young women formed a laughing, chattering semicircle around her. Her dread grew with every step as they walked toward a cleared area at the other end of the room.

"Okay, ladies, are you ready?" Bob Johnson grinned and held up a hand for silence. "On three, Leigh. One…"

Angela brushed past Evelyn Stewart and stepped into the middle of the group of young ladies and women where she would be hidden from view.

"Two…"

Leigh glanced back, planted her feet, and rotated her shoulders.

"Three!"

The bridal bouquet sailed into the air, made a perfect arc and came down straight toward Angela's face. Automatically, she lifted her hands and caught it, then clenched her fingers tight to keep from thrusting it away from her.

The crowd burst into applause and laughter.

Leigh grinned and made a deep curtsey.

"You haven't lost your touch, Leigh!" Barbara Adams grinned as a dozen curious faces turned her way. "She led Harmony High's girls' basketball team to the state championship three years in a row!"

A fresh chorus of cheers and laughter greeted her words. The knot of young single women and girls began to drift apart.

Angela fixed a smile on her face and headed for the door. She couldn't take any more. She was leaving. She would tell Leigh— Her thoughts froze as Hosea stepped out of a group of people and started toward her.

"Angela, may I have a word with you, please?"

No! Oh, Lord, please no!

She couldn't move her feet. She glanced at the doorway, her portal to safety, then lifted her gaze to Hosea. All the love she felt for him was in her eyes. She knew it—and was helpless to stop it.

Hosea stopped, sucked in his breath as their gazes met. Held.

Angela's heart pounded and swelled with unbearable pain. One moment. They might share this one moment, but the love could never be. With a sob, she turned and ran through the door.

"Angela, wait!"

"Pastor Stevens?"

Hosea looked down at the blue-veined hand grasping his arm, then jerked his gaze to the narrow-eyed, pinch-mouthed face of Ina Fleming. Angela's running footsteps echoed in his ears. He removed the hand. "I'll be with you in a minute, Mrs. Fleming. I need to talk to Angela a moment." Turning his back on the woman's disapproving face, he hurried through the door.

Angela was nowhere in sight.

Hosea ran down the hallway to the entrance. The faint beep of a car unlocking sounded outside. He slammed through the double doors and raced across the portico and down the steps. The taillights of Angela's car shone through the falling snow as it sped off down the drive.

"Angela! Angela, don't do this! Stop!" Hosea started after her car at a dead run, but the leather soles of his dress shoes were no match for the slippery snow. He hit a patch of ice, skidded wildly, then— stretching out his hands to protect himself—crashed to the ground. He jerked upright to look for her car. It had disappeared.

"Lord! Oh, Lord, no. *No!*" Hosea's heart filled with an unbearable combination of pain, frustration and fear—love for him wasn't the only thing he had seen in Angela's eyes before she ran away. Stinging pain streaked through his right hand as he pushed against the frozen ground to right himself. It was nothing to what he felt in his heart. He stared down the empty road.

"Please help her, Lord. Please set her free. Oh, Jesus, *please* set her free. I love her so much. So much!"

The words were chunks torn from his heart. Hosea leaned back against the pillar at the end of the driveway and looked down at his right hand. It was scraped, bloodied and swelling. He sucked in a deep, steadying breath of the cold December air, bent down and thrust it in the snow.

She had to hurry! She had to finish before the reception was over. Angela threw the last of the pew bows in the box, swept her gaze over the sanctuary to make sure she hadn't missed anything, picked up the box and ran to her car. That was the last of it. She had kept her promise. Her obligation to Leigh was over. Now she could go home.

Home.

Not any more.

Not now.

Chapter Sixteen

"There you are, Pastor Stevens. I've been waiting."

Hosea stopped just inside the door of the banquet room of The River House and looked into the haughty gaze of Ina Fleming's cold gray eyes. Her thin lips pinched together.

"I'm not accustomed to such rudeness from a minister. Nor such unseemly behavior. It's quite improper for a man in your position to run after a young woman." The woman's eyes narrowed in speculation. "Unless, of course, there was some emergency?"

"Nothing you need concern yourself with, Mrs. Fleming." In spite of his pleasant tone, the woman's nostrils flared and her lips compressed into an angry thin line. Hosea forced his own mouth to lift into a smile. "I'm sorry if you perceived my haste as rudeness, Mrs. Fleming—but I'm here now. What is it you wanted?"

"I wished to speak with you about today's service. I've never witnessed a wedding that so blatantly flaunted tradition. The groom marching down the aisle to the bride—unheard of!''

Ina Fleming's gaze slid to Leigh and her back stiffened. ''I realize, of course, that the modern young women of today often engage in such tasteless displays.'' Her cold gaze came back to Hosea. ''But to allow them to do so in the church—''

''Excuse me, Mrs. Fleming, but if you are lodging a complaint about the Johnsons' wedding, you are speaking to the wrong person. I found the wedding beautiful, tasteful and deeply scriptural.''

Hosea ignored the autocratic lift of the elderly woman's eyebrows at his interruption. He took a deep breath and continued in a low, calm voice. ''And if your complaint is against *me,* for approving it, you need to speak to the church board. I suggest you call them Monday and set up an appointment to discuss the matter. Or, if you would like to learn more about the scriptural basis for the service, I'll be most happy to tell Barbara to set up an appointment for you for private Bible study this week. Just give her a call and settle on the time. I'll look forward to meeting with you. Now, I have duties to perform before we send Phil and Leigh on their way.'' Hosea gave her a polite smile and walked away.

Angela stuffed jeans and sweaters on top of the other clothes, tugged the zipper closed and yanked the suitcase off the bed. It almost pulled her arm from it's socket. She ignored the wrenching pain, slung the strap of her shoe bag over her shoulder and dragged the suitcase down the stairs. Every thunk and bump made her head pound, and her shoulder hurt worse.

She manhandled the heavy bag out the door and pushed and tugged until it fell into the trunk of her car beside the two smaller cases. That was everything.

Her Bible. She couldn't go without her Bible. She slammed the trunk lid closed and ran back to the house.

Angela caught her breath on a sob, switched off the lights and locked the front door. The small night-light in the entryway glowed softly, highlighting the bouquet lying on top of the boxes of wedding decorations randomly stacked just inside the door. Pain ripped through her. *Help me, Jesus. Please help me. I love him so much, I need Your strength to give him up.*

She clutched her Bible close to her heart, stumbled down the steps to her car and drove away.

Her car wasn't in the driveway. The house was dark. A horrible stillness settled over Hosea. She was gone. He pushed the thought away and tried to draw a deep breath to steady himself but the tightness in his chest wouldn't allow it. *Lord, let me be wrong. Please let me be wrong.*

He knew he wasn't. Even as his heart uttered the plea he knew he wasn't.

His hand trembled as he opened the car door and his legs felt like sponge as he crossed Angela's front yard and climbed her porch steps. He pushed the doorbell. It echoed hollowly through the house.

Hosea pushed the bell again, then stepped to the side and looked in the small entrance window. A knot of pain slammed him in the stomach. He closed his eyes to shut out the sight of the bouquet Angela had caught lying on top of the raggedly stacked boxes of wedding decorations. They would never be that way if she was home.

"Father…"

It was all he could say. All he could think. The pain and fear were so keen, so intense, they all but buckled his knees.

Hosea leaned against the house and lifted his hand to wipe across his eyes, to pinch the bridge of his nose. He drew a ragged breath, then another, forcing back the fear, the terrifying, debilitating fear that he had lost her, that she was gone forever.

"And I will betroth thee unto me forever…"

The line of scripture slid into his mind. His heart grabbed hold of it, wrested strength and comfort from it. She was his. God had spoken clearly to him that Angela was to be his bride. His wife forever. The Lord would bring her back to him. Tears welled into his eyes.

"Forgive me, Father. Forgive me for letting fear obliterate faith. For letting my feelings override Your word to me. Forgive me for doubting—for forgetting You love Angela, and that You are working for her good. I believe in You, Lord. But I confess it's hard not knowing where Angela is, or if she's all right. I love her, Lord—and I'm afraid for her. Please, help my unbelief, and help me to rise above the fears of my flesh. I ask it in Your holy name. Amen."

The pressure in his chest lessened as the words of

his prayer echoed through his mind and spirit. Angela was in God's hands. He took a deep breath and pushed away from the wall. "Thank You, Lord. Thank You for loving and caring for her."

Hosea walked down the steps. The snow crunched under his feet as he trudged back to his car. Pain shot through his right hand when he reached automatically for the ignition. He glanced down at the bruised, swollen flesh, then turned the key and pulled over into the turn lane. It was too late tonight, but tomorrow after church he'd go see Sophie. Maybe she would know where Angela had gone.

"Room 112. It's to the left of the elevators."

"Thank you." Angela took the key, pocketed her receipt and picked up her bag. The corridor looked endless. She was so tired. So incredibly tired. Her legs trembled with each step, her hand shook when she unlocked the door. She stepped into the room, threw the security lock in place, twisted the dead bolt, then dropped her bag, kicked off her shoes and fell onto the bed.

If only she could cry. If only she could wash Hosea out of her heart with tears. If only there was another way. If only...if only...if only...

Angela closed her eyes, then promptly opened them again as Hosea's face swam into her mind. Opening her case, she took out her Bible, clutched it to her heart, then laid back against the pillows, pulled the other half of the bedspread over her and stared at the ceiling with dry, burning eyes.

* * *

Hosea couldn't sleep. It wasn't the throbbing in his hand that kept him awake—it was the hollow ache in his heart. He climbed out of bed, pulled on a T-shirt and went to the kitchen.

While the coffee he shouldn't have this time of night brewed, he went to his study for his Bible. Maybe if he read the book of Hosea he would discover something that would help him find Angela. He carried the Bible back to the kitchen, poured his coffee, then sat at the table and began to read. "The word of the Lord that came unto Hosea..."

Chapter Seventeen

Angela's grip on the steering wheel relaxed as she caught a glimpse of log cabins through the pines that paraded beside the lake. She'd found it. Now, if she could just remember where the lodge was located... She drove forward, dappled light flashing through the branches onto the windshield as she made the long curve, and there it was—straight ahead.

A patch of red caught her eye. She slowed, then pulled forward and stopped as she spotted a man in front of the closest cabin. He was leaning on the handle of his snow shovel, squinting toward her. She climbed out and looked at him over the roof of the vehicle.

"Are you Mr. Fields?"

"That's me—Frank Fields." He tugged his hunting cap lower against the biting cold. "What can I do for you?"

"I was wondering if you had a cabin available to rent?"

"Sure do. They're pretty much all empty this time of year." He jerked a thumb toward the small log cabin behind him. "You can have this one if you like—it's already dug out. It'll cost you a hundred dollars for the week, or four hundred for the month. Same amount per week either way."

He touched the brim of his cap and frowned. "You should be wearing a hat, miss. This weather ain't gonna get anything but worse." As if to prove his words a gust of wind blew in from the lake, pelting them with tiny icy pellets.

Angela shivered. She reached up and pulled the collar of her coat up around her neck. "I guess you're right." She gave him a polite smile. "My name's Angela Warren—and I'll take the cabin. Will you take a money order? Or would you prefer a credit card?"

"Money order's fine."

She nodded, then swept her gaze around the snow covered area. "Where should I park my car?"

"You'd best leave it right there where I can plow it out if need be, Miss Warren. There ain't gonna be any traffic comin' by to worry about."

"All right." She glanced beyond him. "Is the cabin open?"

"She's open. I was checkin' the water an' such."

Angela nodded, pushed the trunk release, then grabbed her purse and keys. Another gust of wind blew in from the lake, peppering them with the small icy fragments. She tucked her chin into her collar and struggled against the force of it as she tried to open the trunk.

The man stepped forward, took hold of the heavy

lid with one big, gloved hand and lifted. "I'll get your bags, Miss Warren. You'd best get inside before you catch your death."

She glanced up at him. "All right—I will. Thank you, Mr. Fields." She pulled her overnight bag out of the trunk, then turned toward the cabin.

"Mind your step, miss. There's patches of ice under that covering of snow."

She nodded acknowledgment and started up the cleared path.

"Well, that's about it. Not a lot of luxuries here. And it's pretty lonely this time of year." Frank Fields took off his hunting cap and scratched his balding head. "How'd you find this place, Miss Warren? We're pretty far off the beaten track."

"Our church held a winter retreat here two years ago." Angela reached into her purse and pulled out some money orders. "Do you require a security deposit, Mr. Fields? Or is the rent sufficient?" She glanced up at him. "And what about utilities?"

"Utilities are included in the rent. And that's all I need." He put his hat back on and buttoned his red and black checked jacket. "I don't bother about security deposits. Most people who come up here are a decent sort."

"I'm sure they are." She fished a pen out of her purse, signed her name on the money orders and handed them to him.

"This is enough for a month." He frowned. "You sure you don't want to just take the cabin for a week at a time, Miss Warren? It's the same money either way. An', as I said, it gets pretty lonely up here this time of year.''

"I'm sure, Mr. Fields." She gave him a polite smile. "Thank you for helping me with my luggage."

"Yep." He placed the money orders in the left breast pocket of his jacket and buttoned the flap down over it. "If there's anything you need, just give me a holler when you see me out and around. Or come on up to the lodge if you've a mind to. Mrs. Fields would like that. She gets kind of lonely for female company during the winter."

"I'll keep that in mind."

"Good." His boots clomped against the floor as he walked to the door. "Remember now—the firewood is in this attached shed here at the kitchen door. Don't worry none about how much you use—I'll keep the shed full up." He glanced at her again. "An' I'll bring you some fresh eggs in the morning. We've got two or three hens that are still layin'."

"That would be very nice, thank you."

He nodded, stepped outside and closed the door. Angela watched through the window as he plucked the snow shovel out of the drift, lowered his head into the wind and headed in the direction of the lodge.

Well that was that. At least for the next month. She took a deep breath and looked around the kitchen. Mr. Fields was right. There weren't a lot of luxuries, but it was clean and pleasant. Her gaze drifted over the pine cupboards, quarry-tile counter top, and dark-blue-and-white woven curtains. There was a candle in the window. Tears stung her eyes.

How foolish! Her life was in shambles and she went

weepy over a candle in a window. Angela blinked the moisture away, took off her coat and hung it over one of the mismatched wood chairs surrounding the table.

Icy pellets beat against the windowpane and the wind moaned and whistled, blowing away the dreary gray light of late afternoon as she flipped on the overhead light and began to unpack her groceries.

Chapter Eighteen

"Come in."

Hosea opened the door a crack. "I'm not a nurse, Miss Sophie, are you decent?" There was a throaty laugh.

"It wouldn't matter much if I wasn't, would it?"

"You never can tell." Hosea stepped inside. "I'm single, you know." He gave the elderly woman a grin that brought out that sexy laughter full force. He shook his head and crossed to her chair. "You must have driven men insane, Miss Sophie."

"I did all right."

The look she slanted up at him still had a remnant of feminine allure in it. Hosea grinned. "I'll just bet you did." He held out a puzzle book. "I brought you something."

"Crosswords?"

"Yes."

"Good." She took the book and laid it on the table beside her. "They're my favorite."

"I know. Angela told me."

Sophie shot him a look. "I don't know where she is."

It was too sudden. He hadn't been ready for the jolt of pain her words brought. He turned to look out the window. "I wasn't sure you knew she was gone. I didn't want you to worry, so I came to tell you."

"*And* to find out if I know where she took herself off to."

Hosea's chest tightened. He crossed his arms over the ache, leaned against the window frame and looked at her. "Now, how do you figure that?"

She gave an unladylike snort. "That's easy enough." She held up three fingers. "One—" she curled the first finger downward "—Angela has been increasingly upset these last few weeks, and today she called to tell me she had to go away, but she'll stay in touch. She wouldn't say where she was, or when she'll be back.

"Two—" she curled another finger down "—this is Sunday—the day Angela usually comes to see me— and suddenly *you're* here." She gave him a sly look. "You usually visit me on Fridays.

"And, three—" she curled the last finger down "—you love her. And you're worried about her. I can see it in your eyes."

Sophie reached over, took hold of his jacket and gave a little tug. "Come sit down and talk to me, Hosea Stevens. Maybe we can figure something out. I love her, too. And, unlike you, I'm not above a little chicanery to get her back here."

The pressure in Hosea's chest eased a little. It

helped just to be able to talk about his love for Angela to someone. He tilted Sophie's face up with his good hand and leaned down to kiss her dry, wrinkled cheek. "God, bless you, Sophie. I love you."

"Humph! That's what all you men say when you want something. Now, sit down. You're giving me a crick in my neck." She caught his wrist and tugged.

Hosea obediently dropped into the chair beside her.

"That's better." Sophie reached out and gently touched his swollen, discolored knuckles. "First things first." Her eyes brightened with curiosity. "This is the way a hand looks after a fist-fight. So tell me—how did these bruised knuckles get on the hand of a pastor?"

Hosea frowned. "I chased Angela's car down the drive at the restaurant, slid on the ice, and scraped my hand when I fell."

Sophie burst into laughter. "Lord love you, Pastor, you *do* love her! Only love would make you act so foolish. Now, let me tell you what I had in mind...."

Hosea shook his head to clear his mind, and parked the car. A smile touched his lips at the memory as he climbed out into the snow that had been falling steadily all day. That Sophie was something else! It had taken him the better part of an hour Sunday night to dissuade her from her plan to feign serious illness the next time Angela called. She had stubbornly insisted it would bring Angela back.

And it would.

Hosea frowned at the need that shot through him at the thought of seeing her again. He'd had to wrestle his own desire into submission before he could convince Sophie that God's way was best. That if they used subterfuge to bring Angela home she would only resent them for it and run off again. That it would solve nothing.

"Oh, Lord, bless Angela wherever she is. Oh, Jesus, help her. Please help her!"

Hosea's voice broke. She would be gone a week tomorrow, and he'd exhausted every avenue he could think of to find her. He blinked his eyes, stomped the snow from his shoes and shoved through the entrance doors of the church.

"Hi, Pastor. Still snowing, huh?

"Hi, John. Yeah, it's still coming down."

Hosea brushed the snow from the shoulders of his coat and glanced at the boy who was one of the leaders of the teens who were going caroling tomorrow night. "How's practice going?"

"Pretty good." The young man grinned. "So far, I've only messed up my bass part once."

"That *is* good! Keep it up." Hosea gave the teen a manly thump on the arm and headed for his office.

"Oh, Pastor—I forgot!" John turned and jogged backward down the hall. "Some delivery guy brought some packages for you. I had him put them in your office."

"Okay. Thanks, John. Now turn around before you and that door become intimately acquainted."

The teen grinned, saluted, then spun around and disappeared into the sanctuary.

Hosea stooped to pick up a gum wrapper someone had dropped, tossed it into the hall wastebasket on his

way by, then opened his office door. The packages
were stacked on the floor in front of his desk. He
frowned at sight of them. He had to get hold of himself. He couldn't remember ordering anything for the
church—and judging from the size of the boxes he
should remember.

He shrugged out of his coat, flicked on the overhead
light, and ripped the attached envelope off the top box
on the way to his chair. The return address was an
office supply store.

Hosea frowned, leaned back, slit open the envelope,
and unfolded the letter. He didn't remember author-
izing any purchases for the church from that store.
And he certainly hadn't—

His breath caught. He jolted forward, staring at the
signature at the bottom of the brief note. *Angela!* His
heart thudded as he skimmed the message: "Pastor
Stevens, Please deliver these to Cathy when you take
her your gifts. I didn't want to just send them through
the mail. Thank you. Angela Warren"

Hosea let out his breath and read the note again.
Terse, formal, polite—and not a clue as to where Angela was. He crushed the paper into a wad, tossed it
in the wastebasket, then plunked his elbows down on
his desk and dropped his forehead to rest against his
hands.

Angela pulled the cowl neck of her brick-colored
sweater up around her ears, then jammed her gloved
hands deeply into her coat pockets. The weather had
warmed today but it didn't seem to help. Not even the
slanted gold of the sun's rays warmed her.

If you don't eat you're going to make yourself sick, Angela. Your body needs fuel.

Leigh's words echoed through her mind, adding to the unrelenting tension in her chest, the unyielding ache in her heart. She would feel better if she could cry. But her tears had dried up. There was only an overwhelming sadness, and an incredible weariness. She was so tired, but she couldn't rest. She couldn't sleep until exhaustion overcame her. Whenever she closed her eyes she saw Hosea's face.

Angela stepped around a large, dirty, icy chunk of snow that looked as if it had fallen from a vehicle, then stopped and glanced across the frozen lake at the sound of a motor. She stood in the winter sunlight, watching Frank Fields back his pickup truck up to the shed attached to her cabin and begin unloading firewood. He'd been as good as his word—the shed was always full. She was grateful for that. The fires helped, though nothing really warmed her.

Angela turned and started along the road again, the heaviness that was always with her bowing her shoulders. The pines stretched their branches toward her, silently offering her their sappy, prickly cones. The sharp, pungent smell of their needles made her think of Christmas.

Christmas. Last year she had spent Christmas with Leigh's family. Angela frowned, and ripped her mind away from the thought. That was last year—this was now. She was alone again.

She stopped, lifted her head and looked up at the clear, cold winter sky. She would be alone forever. Unless the Lord worked a miracle. Unless He made another way. But why would He do that for someone like her?

Angela's face tightened. She ducked her head into her collar, hunched her shoulders, and started off around the lake again, quickening her steps, trying to outdistance the hurt—to leave behind the memory of a prostitute named Gelina.

Chapter Nineteen

"When I am afraid, I will put my trust in You."

The words of the psalm stabbed deep into Angela's heart. She *was* afraid. More afraid than she had ever been. Afraid of the long, lonely years ahead now that she knew what might have been. And she *did* trust the Lord. It's just that, in this situation, there was nothing He could do. No. God could do anything! There was nothing He would want to do. God wouldn't want a minister of His word tainted by the filth of an ex-prostitute.

Angela laid her Bible on the seat beside her, rubbed her aching temples, and rose to put another log on the fire. Her face felt hot from the flames, but for some reason she couldn't get warm. She shivered her way to the kitchen, poured herself another cup of tea and went back to curl up in the corner of the couch.

She should pray. She knew she should pray for the Lord's will to be done so Hosea would be free of her, but she didn't have the strength, not yet. She had heard

him calling her. Had looked into her rearview mirror
and seen him running after her. That image was
burned into her mind. Now, there was a tiny part of
her heart that wouldn't accept there would be no miracle for them.

"Oh, Father God, be patient with me. I have a foolish, *foolish* heart."

Angela put her cup down on the table beside her,
leaned her head against the couch back and closed her
eyes. The thought of God taking Hosea's love for her
away was terrifying. Somehow, just knowing he loved
her—even if she never saw him again—made her less
alone.

"Forgive me my weakness, Lord, but I've never
had anyone love me before, and…and just the thought
of it—" Tears squeezed out from under Angela's
closed eyelids, wetting her lashes. "I love him, Lord.
And I never want to hurt him. I know I have to give
him up. I just need a little more time."

The tears rolled down her cheeks. Angela drew a
shuddering breath and wiped them away. "Please help
me, Lord. Forgive me my selfishness, and—and let
Thy will be done."

There. She'd said it. Angela opened her eyes and
lifted her gaze to the window, seeking distraction from
her painful thoughts. It was snowing again. The large,
fluffy flakes piling up in the corners of the windows.
Tomorrow was Christmas. Had Sophie gotten her
package? Would she like the robe and slippers? The
creamy Citrus Splash body butter that would moistur-
ize and soften her dry skin?

Angela rubbed her fingers across her forehead to

ease the dull throb, took a sip of tea and picked up the Bible. "In God, whose word I praise, in God I trust…"

Trust. She had trusted Cathy's packages to Hosea's care. Angela dropped the Bible onto the cushion and surged to her feet. Why did every thought have to turn to Hosea! She had to be done with him! She had to sell her house and move to—to where?

"Where, Lord? Where do I go? I have no one—"

Angela's voice broke. Her head throbbed and her chest hurt. She had to be done with the pain and the indecision. She would call a real estate agent and put her house on the market. Tim Balinger. Yes, she would walk to the lodge and call Tim Balinger and make the arrangements.

And then?

Tears gushed from her eyes. And then she would get a United States map, close her eyes, and point.

Angela gasped for air. The constriction in her chest was becoming unbearable. She could hardly breathe. She needed fresh air! She shoved the screen in front of the fire and ran to get her coat and boots.

Hosea lifted two of the packages from the trunk, slammed the lid closed and started across the parking lot.

"Hi, Pastor Stevens!"

"Hello, Cathy." Hosea smiled as the teenager ran across the intervening space and skidded to a stop in front of him. "How are you? How's school?"

"It's great! I love college. Want some help with

those?'' She nodded toward the large packages he held in his arms.

''No, thanks. They're pretty heavy for you. I can manage. You just lead the way.''

''Okay.'' Cathy laughed and started toward the building. ''I've been watching for you. You made good time in this snow.''

Hosea nodded and followed her through a set of double doors. ''The interstate isn't bad. The plows are keeping up with the downfall.''

''That's good.'' Cathy gestured to the right. ''The visitor's lounge is this way.''

Hosea stomped the snow from his feet and followed her into the spacious room. There was a fake tree with inexpensive plastic ornaments dangling from its branches in the corner. He set the packages on the floor, then looked up and smiled. ''There are a couple more things in the car. I'll be right back.''

When he returned, he doffed his jacket and sat down facing her. ''Dorms are a lot quieter than when I was in college.''

Cathy swept her gaze around the room. ''It's not like this normally. Most everyone has gone home for Christmas break. Usually you can't hear yourself think for the noise.''

''Right. I should have thought of that.'' His gaze met hers. ''Do you want to talk about your dad, Cathy? Have you had any news?''

Her eyes filled. ''No. Just what I told you on the phone. The last time I tried to call home the phone was disconnected. I called the landlord and he said Dad had gone. He didn't know where. The apartment's been rented to someone else. He—he told me not to bother him again. That as far as he was concerned it was 'goodbye to rubbish.'''

"I'm sorry, Cathy." Hosea's voice warmed with compassion. "Are you making it through this all right? Do you need anything?" He smiled. "I know you're doing well academically—your grades are better than mine were. But how are you doing personally?"

"I'm all right." Cathy looked down and brushed some clinging snow from the bottom of one leg of her jeans. "I really enjoy college. And I've made some good friends." She looked up and smiled at him. "A couple of them asked me to go home with them for the holidays, but…" She looked toward the door and lowered her voice. "There's another girl here who's unable to go home, too, so I decided to stay with her."

"That's very thoughtful and generous of you, Cathy. I'm proud of you."

"Thanks." She flushed at his praise and looked away. "I thought maybe Miss Warren would be coming with you.

He had expected it, but the hurt took his breath for a moment anyway. "Not this time. She's out of town. That's why she asked me to bring you her gifts along with mine." He noted the disappointment that clouded her eyes. "I know Christmas isn't until tomorrow, but would you like to open some of these gifts now?"

Her eyes widened. "Could I?"

Hosea grinned. "Sure. You might need some help with a couple of them. Here start with this one." He shoved one of the big boxes toward her. "These little ones are off-limits till Christmas morning."

Cathy picked up the card attached to the ribbon. "It's from Miss Warren."

Hosea nodded, his throat too painfully tight to speak at the thought of the terse instructions that had arrived along with the packages.

"It's a computer!" Cathy's eyes spurted tears.

"Hey! You're not supposed to get a computer wet, Cathy." That earned him a smile. Hosea blinked his own eyes and shoved the next box over to her. She couldn't see to untie the ribbon. He pulled out his jackknife and sliced through it.

"And a monitor. Oh, she shouldn't have."

"Well, a computer isn't much good without one." Hosea cleared his throat. "Here you go." He handed her the next package.

She read the tag and looked up at him with swimming eyes. "This is from the church."

He forced a grin. "Yeah, I know."

"But they didn't have to—a *scanner!*"

"Oops. Wrong package. Here."

Cathy wiped the tears from her cheeks and read the next card. "Another one from the church?" She tore the paper from the next package. "A jet printer! Oh, Pastor…"

Hosea patted her shoulder, then handed her a box of tissues that were sitting on a table under the window. He cleared his throat, wiped his own eyes and jammed the tissue in his pocket as a tall, slender, dark-haired girl with brown eyes stepped through the doorway and stopped at sight of him. He rose to his feet.

"Well, hello." The girl's voice was well modulated, cultured.

Cathy twisted toward the doorway. "Hi, Diane." She gave an audible sniff. "This is my pastor…Pastor Stevens. He brought me the Christmas presents Miss Warren, and my church back home got me." She looked up at him. "Pastor, this is my friend…Diane Whitford."

"Hello, Diane." Hosea smiled, at her. "It's nice to meet you."

She smiled and swept her gaze over the presents on the floor. "Wow! Looks like you hit the jackpot, Cathy."

Hosea smiled at the comment and shifted his gaze back to Cathy. "Will you need help getting these things to your room and hooking them up, Cathy?"

Diane glanced his way. "I can hook them up for her. I don't have anything else to do tomorrow."

Cathy glanced at him and grinned. "Diane's a computer whiz."

Hosea fastened his gaze on the young woman as she dropped into the chair across from him. She was smiling, but there was the same sadness in her eyes there was in Cathy's. He resumed his own seat.

"Well if you're free tomorrow, Diane, there shouldn't be any problem with your spending Christmas Day with Cathy and me." He smiled as Cathy jerked her head up and gaped at him. "Don't look so surprised. We all have to eat sometime." He glanced back at Diane. "Would you join us?"

Cathy surged to her feet. "Oh, Pastor, that would be so much fun!" She hurried over to her friend. "Come on, Diane. Say you'll come."

"I don't know, Cathy, I—"

"Please?"

Diane looked from Cathy, to him, and back to Cathy again. A slow smile spread across her face. "All right."

Cathy gave a squeal and threw her arms around Diane in an excited hug.

Hosea let out the breath he had been holding and rose to his feet. "That's great. I'll come get you early tomorrow morning, say eight o'clock?" He grabbed his jacket and pulled it on. "And pack a bag. I'll make sleeping arrangements for you. It's too far to come back the same day." He lifted a hand in farewell and hurried from the room. He had a phone call to make.

"Hi, Barbara. It's me." Hosea checked his mirror, moved into the passing lane, and accelerated past a slow moving tractor-trailer. "I know you're on vacation, and I apologize for calling you at home, but I need a huge favor."

"Sure, Pastor, what is it?"

He blew out a breath of relief. "I need your help in organizing an impromptu dinner for Christmas Day."

"*What?*"

He yanked the phone away from his ear at her startled yelp, and passed another truck while he gave her time to become accustomed to the idea.

"Barbara?" He got no further. His tentative query brought her back to life.

"Pastor, organizing a dinner takes time. Christmas is *tomorrow*. I mean no disrespect, but have you lost your mind?"

Hosea laughed. "No, I think I still qualify as sane. Listen, Barbara, I wouldn't ask this of you, but Cathy Anders and a very lonely, very hurt friend need someplace to go, and someone to be with, on Christmas. And, since I certainly can't have them alone with me in my home, I thought a dinner at The River House, and a motel for them for the night would fill the bill."

Hosea ignored the ache thought of The River House caused and plunged on. "I don't dare wait until I get back to call the restaurant for reservations or try to locate a room." He heard something that sounded decidedly like a snort.

"Oh, Pastor—you're a wonderful person and we all love you, but, at times, you are such a single man."

Now what did that mean? "I beg your pardon?" Barbara's laughter burst out of the phone and tickled his eardrum.

"I mean, why a motel? Why not with the Bakers? With their boys unable to come home, I know Loretta would love to have someone to fuss over for the holidays."

"That's a wonderful idea!" Hosea smiled into the phone. "You're a jewel, Barbara. Call the Bakers and let me know what they say. And if they don't agree—"

"I'll find someone else."

"Right. Thanks, Barbara. This is all above and beyond the call of duty. I won't forget it."

She laughed again. "Don't worry. I won't let you. I'm already hatching schemes and making plans."

Hosea laughed. "Just don't get too creative. I'll talk with you later. And thanks again." He rang off.

The Bakers. An older couple whose sons were in the military and couldn't come home for the holidays. What could be better? Hosea frowned. He should have thought of them, but he hadn't. And it wasn't because he was single. He was giving too much thought to his own problems. "Forgive me, Lord. And thank You for opening my eyes to my own selfishness. I haven't been giving my all to caring for Your children. Please help me, by Your grace, to do better. In Your name I ask it. Amen"

A sign advertising the motel where he had reserved a room flashed by. He still had fifteen miles to go. He selected a praise CD and popped it into the player.

The fresh air wasn't helping. She was feeling more miserable by the minute. Angela pulled the collar of her coat up around her ears and tucked her gloved hands into her pockets. It didn't help. She couldn't stop shivering. She lowered her head against the wind and tried to catch her breath. The cold air seared her lungs—made her cough. Pain shot through her head. The muscles in her chest tightened around the ache that settled there.

Angela wiped her tearing eyes, lifted her head and looked down the road that wound around the lake to the lodge. She could barely make out the building through the heavily falling snow. Her heart sank. She'd never make it that far. She'd have to go back. She'd call the real-estate agent tomorrow. No—tomorrow was Christmas.

Helpless tears bubbled to the surface and froze on her cheeks. She burrowed deeper into her coat and started back toward the cabin, then sagged against the trunk of a nearby tree to rest. She felt so weak. She forced herself erect and doggedly put one foot in front of the other. The blowing snow clung to the wool of her coat and dribbled down her neck making the shivering worse. She brushed off her collar and trudged on.

Nothing had ever looked quite so welcome as the cabin door when she reached it. Angela pulled it open and warm air rushed out to meet her. She brushed her coat free of the clinging snow and stepped inside. Her strength was gone. She took off her boots, added wood to the fire, then curled up on the couch. A fit of coughing wracked her body. She pulled a crocheted afghan over herself and closed her eyes.

Chapter Twenty

The shaking woke her. Angela forced her eyes open and stared into darkness. The fire was out. She swung her feet to the floor, then grabbed her head and moaned. When things stopped spinning, she pushed to her feet. Chills wracked her. Her joints ached. Her skin hurt.

She clamped her jaws together to stop the chattering of her teeth, closed the flue of the fireplace, then staggered to the bathroom and shivered her way through a hot shower. When she had toweled herself off, she struggled into her warmest pajamas and, bracing herself against the wall, headed for the bedroom. She knew she should eat something, but she didn't have the strength to walk to the kitchen. She wasn't sure she could make it to the bed. She got down on her hands and knees and crawled.

The hands were reaching for her. Big hands with black hair on the knuckles of the long thick fingers...

"No. No!" Angela flailed her arms out into the air, her hands searching, groping.

...The door was locked. She rattled the knob, and beat on the door with her fists. A man laughed. The hands came closer....

Angela screamed and curled her body into a tight ball beneath the covers.

...Help me! Somebody, please help me! The door was pulled open and she fell into Hosea's arms.

Angela jerked upright, shivering and sobbing. Moonlight poured in the window, and dark shadows surrounded her. She sank back down onto her pillow, her heart pounding. It was only the nightmare. Thank God, it was only the nightmare. But this time it had been different. This time Hosea had rescued her. What did it mean?

Angela pulled the covers up around her neck and ran her tongue over her dry, cracked lips. She hadn't had the nightmare for years. It must have been brought on by the fever. She was probably dehydrated. She needed water. She shuddered as her thoughts returned to the nightmare.

Hosea. Oh, Hosea, if only things could be different, she thought.

Angela slid out of bed, pulled off a blanket and wrapped it around her shoulders. The room whirled. Nausea rose into her throat. She couldn't do it. She couldn't walk. And there was no one to help her. *Oh, Lord, I'm so tired of being alone.*

Hot, salty tears stung her eyes. Shivering and shaking, Angela leaned against the edge of the bed for support, then sank to her hands and knees and began to crawl to the bathroom sink. She was halfway across the room when her strength gave out and everything went black.

Angela! Hosea bolted upright in bed, his pulse racing, his heart pounding with fear. Something was wrong with Angela!

"Oh, Lord…oh, dear Jesus, protect her! Help her, Lord!"

He threw off his blankets and leaped to his feet, more frightened than he had ever been in his life. His mind filled with all manner of horrible, terrifying possibilities, he began to pace the room and pray.

The water felt so good to her parched mouth and throat. Angela took another drink, then felt herself lowered to the softness of a pillow. A cool cloth was wiped gently across her face and left to rest on her forehead. The throbbing in her temples lessened. She tried to open her eyes, to see her benefactor, but she couldn't force them open.

"She gonna be all right? Should I try to get her to the hospital?"

Hospital! That was Frank Fields talking. Angela struggled again to open her eyes. She had to tell him not to take her to a hospital. Leigh's name was listed as the emergency contact on her health insurance card. They would call her!

"The truck might make it, but it'd be better to wait till the plows go through." Frank's voice sounded gruff with sleep. "I'd hate to get stuck somewhere."

Lord, don't let them take me anywhere! She tried to protest. But all that came out was a weak moan.

"Hush now, Frank. You're making her fretful." A blanket was tucked more snugly around her shoulders. Angela shivered beneath its warmth. "She took the aspirin and water, and that's the most important thing. I think she'll be all right as long as she can drink water. I'll watch her close. If it's the flu, there's nothing they can do at the hospital that I can't do right here, anyway. I'll give them a call and see what they say as soon as the phone is working again."

Angela stopped struggling. It would be all right. She could stay here.

"Want me to build a fire, Greta? Or do you need somethin' else done?"

Greta. Frank's wife? She couldn't remember. Her brain felt like it was full of cotton.

"A fire would be wonderful. But, first you can go get me some clothes and bring back some of that chicken soup I made for supper." There was the sound of movement. A chair scraped across the floor. It squeaked in protest as it took someone's weight. "Soup's good and strengthening, and this young lady looks peaked and worn-out to me. I'll feed her some of it when she wakes. When you come back you can sleep on the couch while I sit with her."

Lights flickered against her eyelids, went dark, then flickered on again.

"Uh-oh. I'd better bring the lanterns, and some candles, too. Looks like the power is goin' out next. I'm surprised we haven't lost it yet. It's a regular blizzard out there. Be back as quick as I can."

Boots clomped against the floor. A door opened and shut.

A blizzard. Angela gave an inward sigh and stopped fighting the exhaustion. She was safe. They couldn't take her…anywhere…in a…blizzard….

The sledding party had seemed endless—and the meal with the Bakers had taken forever. But Cathy and Diane were now safely ensconced at the Bakers' home until New Year's and he was free until tomorrow afternoon.

Hosea drove down the all but deserted streets of Harmony, catching a glimpse here and there of families gathered together in their living rooms, talking, playing games, the lights of their Christmas trees glowing behind them. His hands tightened on the wheel. This was the worst Christmas of his life. He couldn't remember ever having such a horrendous day. His fear for Angela was a weight on his heart and a cluster of tight knots in his stomach. Nothing eased it.

Hosea frowned and flicked on his windshield wipers. It was starting to snow—those big snowflakes that clumped together and weighted down tree branches and power lines. Must be the blizzard that had been raging up in the mountains for the last twenty-four hours was headed their way.

The snow came faster. The streetlights turned into faint, indistinct golden glows. Hosea increased the speed of his wipers, clicked his lights onto low beam, and headed for the church to pick up the SUV. He'd need it if he received any emergency calls. His car would soon be useless in this storm. The knots in his stomach twisted tighter. Was Angela somewhere in this storm? Was she driving in it?

"Father God, if Angela is in this storm please protect her. Give her a safe, warm haven, Father, and keep her from all harm. I ask it in Jesus' name. Amen."

Hosea frowned. The prayer didn't help. His fear for Angela's safety was eating away at his faith, like a rat gnawing a hole in a wall. If only he knew she was all right! If only he *knew*.

"Well, hello."

The woman had a round face, gray hair and a lovely smile. Angela blinked her eyes to clear her vision and darted her gaze around the room. Yes, she was still in the cabin. Her brow furrowed. She looked back at the woman. "Wh-who are you? Why are you here?" There was an edge of panic to her voice. Her frown deepened. She knew better than to show fear.

"I'm Greta. I'm Frank's wife, dear."

The woman smiled again, and Angela's panic dissolved. She ran her tongue over her dry lips, and was immediately offered water. Nothing had ever tasted as good. She smiled her thanks.

"Are you feeling up to some chicken soup, dear? I have some simmering on the stove."

Angela fought back her weariness. "You made chicken soup? How long have you been here, Mrs. Fields?"

"Since three o'clock. But the soup was last night's dinner. And call me Greta, dear."

Angela shot a glance at her alarm clock. It was two o'clock—in the afternoon, judging by the gray light coming in the window. The woman had been with her since the middle of the night. Angela looked back at her. "You've been here all night?"

Greta Fields sat up a little straighter in the chair she had pulled beside the bed. "That's right."

"Why?" Angela tried to make sense of it. "I—I mean, why did you come?"

"Well…" The woman's cheeks turned pink. "I just suddenly woke up with this strong feeling that you were in trouble. So, I made Frank bring me over to check on you." She blew out a gust of air and her color heightened. "I think it was the Lord that woke me."

Angela gave her a weak smile. "Well, thank you for coming." She closed her eyes.

Greta patted her hand and rose to her feet. "You rest, dear, while I go get you some of that soup."

Angela opened her eyes and stared after Greta Fields as she left the room. Had the Lord sent Greta to take care of her? She smiled and let her eyelids drift closed again. It was a lovely thought. It made the weight of despair that rested on her heart feel a little lighter.

Hosea pulled into the garage behind his house and climbed from the SUV. He stepped out into the falling, blowing snow, punched the button to close the overhead door behind him, and trudged to the back entrance.

The wind almost snatched the door from his hand. He manhandled it closed, took off his boots and hung his jacket on a hook to dry. His gloves he tossed on the shelf above.

The storm increased its fury. The wind howled around the windows in his study, plastering them with clinging snow. Hosea crossed to the fireplace, opened the damper and held a lit match to the crumpled-up newspaper. Flames danced upward licking with greedy tongues at the kindling and logs piled on the grate.

The lights flickered. Hosea frowned, crossed to his desk and lifted the phone from its base to call his parents while he could still get through. He punched in their number, plunked himself down on the sofa and crossed his ankles on the coffee table.

''Hello.''

''Hi, Mom, merry Christmas!''

''Hosea! Merry Christmas! We were afraid you'd be too busy to call.''

''I'm never that busy, Mom.'' Hosea smiled. Grown-up or not, there was nothing like your mom's voice to lift you up and make you feel better when you were down. Unless it was her hug. He gripped the phone tighter.

''How is your hand, Hosea? I hope you're not over-using it.''

He chuckled at her immediate ''mom'' reaction. ''My hand's fine—I'm being careful of it.''

''See that you do. And how are you doing, Hosea?''

''I'm okay, Mom.''

''You haven't heard from Angela?''

''No. Not yet.'' He put his feet on the floor and leaned forward. ''Is Dad there?''

''Yes. I'll get him. I love you, Hosea.''

"I love you too, Mom."

Hosea's throat tightened. He surged to his feet and walked over to look out the window. All he could see was snow.

"Hey, Hosea. Merry Christmas! I hear on the news you might be visited by that blizzard that's been raging across those magnificent mountains out there."

"Hey, Dad! Merry Christmas to you, too." Hosea turned his back to the window and leaned against the wall. "I think the outer fringe of the blizzard is here already. It started a little while ago. I had to get the SUV from church to get home."

"Well, if you have to be out and about, drive safe. Hosea, your mom said you didn't sound good. She's right. We're concerned about you, son."

Hosea's chest filled. He pushed away from the wall and walked toward the fireplace. "There's no reason to be concerned, Dad. I've just had a hard day because of Angela."

"Something specific?"

There was a sharp pop. A glowing cinder flew out into the room and landed on the hardwood floor. Hosea kicked it back into the fireplace. "No. It's just that I don't know where she is, or if she's all right, and it's killing me! I can't seem to get a grip on the situation."

"Have you given her to the Lord, son?"

Hosea's brows knit together in a frown. He plunked back down on the couch. "Of course I've given her to the Lord, Dad. That's the first thing I did."

"Then trust Him, son. He knows what He's doing. Try looking at this as if you were counseling—"

Hosea stared at the dead phone in his hand, then tossed it onto the couch beside him and leaned back to stare up at the ceiling.

"Lord, my dad said I should look at this situation as if I were a counselor, but I can't do that. I can't be objective. I love Angela, Lord. I love her. And not knowing where she is, or if she's all right, is tearing me up. I need Your wisdom, guidance, and—"

"Have you given her to the Lord, son?"

His father's words stabbed to the very marrow of his being. Tears sprang to Hosea's eyes. He slid off the couch to his knees and buried his face in his hands.

"Forgive me, Lord. Oh, Jesus, forgive me! I've trusted Angela to Your care with my head, but not with my heart. I've been holding on, Lord…wanting to find her…wanting to minister to her…wanting to help her, so I can have her for my own. Oh, Lord, forgive me. Please forgive me. I give her to You. With all my heart, Lord, I give Angela to You. She's Your child, have Your way in her life. Even if I never see her, again, Lord. Even if I never see her again. Have Your way."

Hosea crossed his arms on the couch cushion and pressed his forehead against them. He stayed on his knees a long time. At last he pushed to his feet and went to stare at the darkness outside the window.

I might never see her again. She might be lost to me forever. Oh, how that possibility hurt! Hosea cringed inwardly. That's what he had been afraid of— that's why he'd held on and not truly given Angela to the Lord before. Where was his faith?

He leaned against the wall and closed his eyes. He

didn't have an answer. He'd never felt so helpless in his life. He frowned, and took a deep breath. There's no profit in standing here feeling sorry for yourself, he told himself. Do something.

He opened his eyes, shoved away from the wall and went to prepare his list of scriptures for Sunday's sermon.

Chapter Twenty-One

What was that smell? Was someone cooking? Angela gave an appreciative sniff and opened her eyes. All was blackness, except for a thin thread of dim light at the edge of the bedroom door. A murmur of voices came from the other room. Her heart lurched with fear, and then she remembered Frank Fields and his wife had come to take care of her. Warmth settled around her heart. Her pulse slowed to normal. How kind of them to come.

Angela closed her eyes and took inventory. She needed water—her mouth was dry as a desert. Other than that, she felt much better. Slowly, she turned onto her side, reached for the lamp on the nightstand, and pushed the slide button. Nothing. The electricity must be off. Great! She'd have to make her way to the bathroom in the pitch-black.

Angela gathered her strength and pushed to a sitting position. The cold air made her shiver. She pulled a blanket off the bed, wrapped it around her shoulders and got shakily to her feet. Her knees folded. She caught hold of the bed post and held on. The exertion wore her out. She sat down on the edge of the bed and leaned against the post waiting for her strength to return.

The door opened.

"You're up!" Greta Fields stopped short, gaping at Angela in surprise. The flame of the candle she held in her hand flickered, then steadied.

"Sort of." Angela grimaced at her dry, raspy voice and squandered her returning strength on a smile. "I needed a drink of water, but this is as far as I got."

"I'm not surprised." Greta hurried forward and placed the candle on the nightstand. Light illuminated a glass of water sitting there. She picked it up and offered it to Angela.

The cold wetness felt wonderful sliding down her throat. But it increased her shivering.

"Why you're about to shake yourself apart! And no wonder—it's like a refrigerator in here."

Angela flinched when Greta reached toward her, but the woman only pulled the blanket more tightly around her shoulders. Her hands left little spots of warmth where they touched her cold skin.

Greta frowned. "It's my fault. I should have thought to leave the door open. With the electricity out, the only heat is from the fireplace." She looked toward the door, then back at Angela. "Do you feel well enough to lie on the couch? It would be warmer for you."

"I think so. But I don't know if I can walk—" Greta's hand on her shoulder stopped her.

"Frank!"

Angela's landlord appeared at the door. "You need somethin'?"

Greta nodded. "I want you to carry Miss Warren out to the couch. It's too cold in here."

"Oh, but—" Angela's protest died as she was scooped up, blanket and all, and carried from the room. Frank deposited her gently on the couch. "Thank you, Mr. Fields."

Greta tucked the quilt she had brought from the bedroom around Angela legs and smiled at her. "Call him Frank, dear."

"All right. And I'm Angela."

Greta smiled, and placed Angela's bed pillow behind her head. "That's a lovely name. And certainly appropriate for the day. Now, you rest. I'm going to get—"

"Appropriate for—" Angela's eyes widened. "It's Christmas! It's Christmas night, isn't it?" She made the calculations. "Oh, I've ruined your holiday. I'm so sorry."

"You've nothing to be sorry for, dear." Greta bent and put her arms around Angela. "The blizzard has us house-bound, and this is a perfectly lovely way to spend Christmas. Usually, Frank and I are all alone. We have no children, so this is a wonderful blessing for us." She kissed Angela's cheek and straightened. "Now, you need something to eat to build up your strength. I'll be right back." She headed for the kitchen.

Angela sank back against the pillow and lifted her hand to cover the spot on her cheek where Greta had planted her kiss. Was that what a mother's kiss felt like? She looked over at Frank, who was busy adding logs to the fire. When he had carried her—she hadn't been afraid. Was that gentle strength the way a father's arms felt?

Angela blinked and swallowed hard, forcing a smile as Greta came back with a bowl of soup and a piece of buttered bread. The bread looked homemade.

"Here you are, dear." Greta plumped and pushed Angela's pillow to help her sit up straighter, then turned and motioned toward the open Bible on the stand beside the big easy chair. "Keep reading, Frank. I'll be right back. I'm going to get us all some tea."

Frank glanced at Angela. "You don't mind if I read from your Bible?"

"Please do." She took a spoonful of chicken soup. It was delicious. Suddenly, she was ravenously hungry. She took another spoonful.

"All right." Frank pulled glasses from his pocket and propped them on the bridge of his ample nose. "Now where was I? Let's see…oh yeah." He cleared his throat. "But the angel said to them, Do not be afraid. I bring you good news of great joy that will be for all the people. Today in the town of David a Savior has been born to you; he is Christ the Lord."

Angela listened to the beautiful words of hope as she ate a few more bites of the soup then lowered the bowl to her lap. She couldn't eat any more, and she couldn't manage the bread. She was just too weak and tired. Peace settled over her, easing the pressure in her chest. The message of hope was for all people. That included her. No matter what she was.

She sighed and laid back against the pillow. It was Christmas, and she was not alone. The Lord had sent these wonderful people to take care of her in her need. That was a miracle. A true miracle. The Lord had worked a miracle...for her.

Angela's eyelids drifted closed. Her breathing slowed. Frank read on. Greta took the soup bowl from her lap. It was the last thing she heard before sleep claimed her.

There was a wall. A huge, endless wall made of stones. She couldn't climb over it, couldn't dig under it, and couldn't go around it. Tears filled Angela's eyes. She had to get to the other side. She just had to! All the Lord had for her was over there!

Angela whimpered, and began to thrash around under the quilt.

She began to run along the wall, and then she saw it—a door. It was so small compared to the vastness of the wall she had almost missed it. She rushed over and tried the knob. It was locked. No. No! She had to get through the door! She rattled the knob, beat the door with her fists, and kicked at it with her feet. Her hands bloodied. Her feet bruised. She collapsed against the door sobbing. "Help me! Somebody help me!" The door was pulled open from the other side. She fell into Hosea's arms.

"Shhh, dear. It's all right." Greta's warm hand touched her forehead. Her work-roughened fingers brushed away the tears seeping from under Angela's lashes.

"Oh, gracious heavenly Father, You who know all

things, help this Your child in her hour of need. Let her know Your all encompassing love, Your unsurpassing peace, and Your everlasting mercy. Meet her need, Father God, whatever it may be. I ask this is Jesus' name. Amen.''

Angela quieted. It was a beautiful prayer.

Chapter Twenty-Two

"Phil! Leigh! Welcome home!" Hosea rushed around his desk and enveloped his two friends in a huge bear hug. "How was Europe?"

"Old."

"Inspiring!"

Hosea laughed. "I guess it's both those things." His smile faded as he stepped back and looked at them. "Is something wrong?"

Leigh nodded. "I couldn't wait to see Angela. We just came from her house." She fastened her gaze on Hosea's eyes. "What's happened? Where is she?"

His joy evaporated. He shook his head. "I don't know, Leigh. No one does."

She stared at him a long moment, then sank down into one of the chairs in front of his desk. "How long has she been gone?"

Hosea took a breath and sat down on the corner of his desk facing her. "Since your reception."

Leigh's face blanched. "I thought it might be something like that. I saw the bouquet on top of the boxes of decorations in the entrance hall."

Hosea leaned forward and laid his hand on her arm. "I'm sorry, Leigh. I didn't want you to find out that way she was gone."

"What difference does that make?" Leigh's voice broke. She got up and walked over to look out the window.

Phil started after her.

"Better not come any closer, Phil." She faced him with tear filled eyes. "I haven't decided if I want to cry, or kick something."

"I'm here for you either way, honey."

Phil wrapped his arms around her. Leigh rested her head against his shoulder for a moment, then took a deep breath and turned in his arms to face Hosea. Her eyes scanned his face. "So, are we still doing nothing about this?"

There was a hint of anger behind the words.

"Leigh…"

Hosea held up his hand. "It's all right, Phil." He met Leigh's gaze. "There's nothing we can do but pray, Leigh. We don't know where she is. But—"

"What about Sophie? Surely she told Sophie where she is."

Hosea shook his head.

"It's been three weeks!"

"I know." He couldn't quite mask the pain that was with him every waking moment—and often in his sleep. In spite of his best effort it crept into his voice.

Leigh stepped out of Phil's arms. "I'm sorry, Hosea. I know you love Angela." She laid her hand on his. "As hard as this is for me, it has to be horrible for you." She glanced back at her husband, then rushed back to his arms. "I can't even imagine how I would feel if Phil disappeared—I don't want to."

Hosea gave the newlyweds a rueful smile. "It's not a situation I would recommend. But—" He reached out and tapped the Bible on his desk "—God is in control, and He knows where Angela is. He's watching over her—I'm convinced of that. And if we love her, then we have to trust Him to do what's best for her."

"That's what you said before. And now she's disappeared!" Leigh's eyes filled with tears.

Hosea's heart swelled with compassion for the young woman who had lost her best friend. "I know, Leigh. But just because we don't understand what the Lord is doing doesn't make what I said any less true. It just makes it…harder." Hosea swallowed back his own pain. "Walking by faith is not easy—especially when someone you love is involved."

He rose to his feet, walked to his desk chair and sat down. Absently, he reached out and drew his Bible to him. "You know, I've counseled people about walking by faith for years. And, I truly thought I understood it. But the last eight months—especially these last few weeks—have shown me how wrong I was. It's much, *much* harder living it."

Angela tucked her gloved hands in her pockets and walked down the front steps of the lodge to the road

Frank had plowed to her cabin. She was grateful for the exercise the walk provided her. Ever since Greta had nursed her through the flu, she had been on a one-woman campaign to fatten her up—as testified to by the coffee cake she had just been served.

Angela lifted her head and swept her gaze over the tall banks of snow to the dull, gray sky. Snowflakes were beginning to drift down. The lazily floating smattering of snow no longer fooled her. This was the way it had started every day since the blizzard, and there was now over seven feet of snow on the ground. She frowned and burrowed her chin further down in her coat collar. From the looks of things, there would be no relief today from the relentless pounding the weather was giving the area. And no hope of telephone service restored.

Angela slowed her steps. It had been two weeks. She was beginning to think she wasn't supposed to call and put her house on the market. Maybe, for some reason, the Lord— No.

Angela shook her head and smiled. She was starting to think like Greta. Greta saw the Lord's hand in everything. Not that that was a bad thing. She tipped her head back to look at up at the sky again.

"Are you orchestrating all this, Lord? Did you bring all this snow to take out telephone service so I can't call and put my house on the market?"

Her words brought a sudden, intense awareness of the Lord's majesty and power. Angela's smile died. For whatever reason—illness, blizzard, interrupted phone service—she *had* been prevented from calling and selling her house. *Was* there a reason? The Lord had sent Greta and Frank to care for her when she had been too ill to care for herself. That was a miracle—for her. Would the Lord work another one for her? Could there possibly be some way she and Hosea—No. No, the Lord wouldn't want that. She mustn't indulge her heart with such foolish hope.

Angela pushed the thought from her mind and started down the plowed road again. The banks of snow formed high walls on either side of her with the tops of the towering pines showing above them on her left. It was so still and silent, she might have been alone in the world.

Or maybe not.

Angela smiled and looked up at the sound of scraping. Frank was cleaning off her cabin roof again.

"Hey!" Angela waved her arms to get his attention. "Want a good, hot cup of coffee when you're finished up there?"

Frank leaned on his shovel and grinned down at her. "No, thanks." He wiped a snowy sleeve across his sweating brow. "This is definitely not cold work. And I am finished here." He tossed down the shovel, climbed down the ladder leaning against the roof eaves, collapsed it, and shoved it onto the bed of his truck. "Only two more roofs to go."

He climbed into the cab, then looked back at her. "I left two eggs on that little table inside the front door. Didn't want to track up your floor." He slammed the door shut. The truck's motor roared to life. Gray exhaust rose in a small cloud.

''Thank you!''

Frank's hand waved once in acknowledgment as he drove away.

Angela stomped the snow from her boots and went inside. The fire was almost out. She added another log, picked up the eggs and headed for the kitchen to put them away. She had another week in the cabin before her month was up. She would wait until then to call about the house. Meanwhile, she would pray for direction on what to do, and where to go.

A niggling thought that she was being cowardly in putting off the inevitable wormed its way into her mind. Angela ignored it, put water on for tea, and went to hang up her coat.

Hosea dumped his plate of half-eaten supper into the garbage disposal, rinsed his dishes, loaded them into the dishwasher, then went to the living room. He'd lost his appetite—not to mention weight. He frowned down at his jeans. If he lost any more weight he'd have to buy new ones. But, at least, the loss wasn't so noticeable in his suits. That was a blessing. Suits were expensive.

He walked to the piano and sat down, running his hand over the smooth, polished wood. He'd always found solace in music and that comfort had been denied him since he'd injured his hand. Opening the key cover, he flexed the stiffness from his fingers and ran them over the keys in an experimental run. His right hand wasn't as agile as usual but it was better than he had expected. He ran his hands over the keys in another practice run, then began to play giving them free rein. The melody of a favorite chorus filled the room. He sang along, the words a prayer from his heart.

"'May the Spirit of the Living God, descend now on me;

Making my heart pure; Setting my spirit free.

May the power of His presence, change me somehow;

May the Spirit of the Living God, descend upon me now.'"

The sound of his voice faded into the night.

Hosea sat thinking and praying while his hands roamed over the keys, playing chords, picking out notes at random. Suddenly he stiffened. Pain shot through him as he recognized the song his betraying hands were playing. His lips formed the words. "'Let me call you sweetheart; I'm in love—'" His voice broke.

So much for the solace of music.

Hosea yanked his fingers from the keys, closed the cover, and left the room. Striding into his study, he flopped down on the couch and draped his arm over his eyes.

January fifteenth. She's been gone a month today. Oh, Lord, how am I to endure this?

Hosea forced himself to take stock. The constant ache in his heart was still there. The empty, hollow feeling in his gut never left him. But at least the ceaseless turmoil in his spirit was gone. He'd finally gotten the victory over that when he had truly released Angela to the Lord's care. He flinched at the sense of loss that flooded over him.

Would he ever see her again?

Hosea bolted upright with a snarl, and reached for the TV remote. He hated these long, lonely nights! He'd never felt like this before Angela had disappeared. How could you miss something you'd never had so badly? Would it ever stop?

Where was the remote? Hosea shoved aside the newspaper and looked under the couch cushions. Nothing. Where—?

What difference did it make? He didn't want to watch TV, he wanted to find Angela! There had to be something, somewhere, that would lead him to her.

Hosea plowed his hands through his hair and paced the room. Tomorrow he was going to search through the church records for the last six years. Maybe he'd find a clue in them. Maybe he'd find the answer to Angela's whereabouts tomorrow. *Oh, Lord, please help me find the answer tomorrow.*

Two more days. She had come here on the seventeenth of December. Today was the fifteenth of January. A month since Leigh's wedding. A month since—

Angela wrenched her mind from the thought and walked away from the window.

What should she do? She had spent the last month

in almost constant prayer and still had received no sense of direction. All she had was her own tumultuous thoughts and foolish hope. What did God want her to do?

"Oh, Lord, why don't You answer me? Why don't You speak to me as You do to Greta?" Angela's face tightened. She knew the answer to that. *That* was the one thing she was certain of—and that gave her the answer to all the other questions. There was no reason for God to speak. She knew what she had to do.

Angela glanced at her Bible. She didn't have to pick it up and read the verses again—she had memorized the scripture from the book of Corinthians. "Love is patient, love is kind. It does not envy, it does not boast, it is not proud. It is not rude, it is not self-seeking...."

Angela stopped quoting and closed her eyes. There was more, but that was the one. *Love is not self-seeking.* If she went back—if she allowed Hosea to love her, to...to marry her, it would destroy him. It would fulfill her own selfish needs, but it would destroy Hosea's calling as a pastor—and that would destroy Hosea the man. She could never do that. She loved him.

That strange, numb, hollow feeling she'd been experiencing came over her again. Angela welcomed it. She was careful not to probe it or disturb it. It protected her from the pain—oh, so much pain—that lay just under the surface.

She picked up her Bible and curled up in the corner of the couch, hugging it to her chest. She would give herself these last two days. Two foolish days of hope, and then she would make the call. She would put her house on the market and arrange for a moving company to place her things in storage. Then she would get in her car and drive. Where she went didn't matter. She had no one to go to. She would just stop when she was somewhere far, far away.

The hollow, numb feeling exploded in a burst of pain so intense Angela gasped and fell forward. She curled into a fetal position around the Bible, buried her face in the couch cushion, and wept.

"We got your message." Phil stopped just inside the door. "What's going on?"

Hosea looked up from the stack of papers he was going through. "I need your help."

"I guess." Leigh swept her gaze over the office. "What a mess!"

"I know." Hosea blew out a breath and plowed his hands through his hair. "I've been going through six years of church files to see if I can find a clue to Angela's whereabouts. It has to be here."

"Okay." Phil tossed his jacket on a chair and rubbed his palms together. "How can we help?"

"I need you to do me a favor." Hosea yanked another file out of a half-empty drawer and started going through it. "The Bakers are bringing Cathy and Diane over in few minutes. I'm supposed to drive them back to Middleton, but I don't have time. I have to go through these files today. Could you take them back to school for me?"

"Sure. No problem. Leigh got Dr. Waters to cover for her when we got your message."

Hosea flashed Leigh a smile. "Thanks. I appreciate it. This is really important, or—"

"Hi, Pastor. Hi, Mr. and Mrs. Johnson! This is my friend Diane."

Leigh smiled at the teenagers standing in the doorway. "Hi, Cathy. Hello, Diane, It's nice to meet you. Have you girls been having a good time with the Bakers?"

"Oh, it's been great!" Cathy beamed at them all. "But the best was sledding with them a few days ago. I hadn't been sledding since the church took the youth group to those cabins up in the mountains two years ago. Remember what a good time we all had on that retreat, Mrs. Johnson?" She laughed. "You guys and Mr. Black and Miss Warren got into that snowball fight and—"

"What did you say, Cathy?" Hosea put down the file and came around the table toward her. "What about Miss Warren and cabins in the mountains?" His heart was going like a trip-hammer. That was it! He was sure of it. And so were Leigh and Phil if the stunned look on their faces was any indication. "Where are the cabins?"

Cathy shrugged. "I don't know, Pastor. I—"

"They're six hours west of here." Phil headed toward a closet at the end of the room. "We still have a map with the route marked on it...." He opened the door, rummaged through a box of papers, then turned and handed a map to Hosea. His face spread in a huge grin. "I saved it because a few of us were planning to go back up there to try our hand at fishing in the lake."

Joy spurted through Hosea. He slapped Phil on the back, grinning so wide he thought his face would split. "Well, praise God, Phil! Praise God, you love to fish!"

"Amen to that!"

Hosea laughed and stepped aside as a laughing, sobbing Leigh launched herself through the air into her husband's arms.

Chapter Twenty-Three

Hosea grabbed the bag he had packed and ran downstairs. All main roads throughout the state had been reported clear but he was taking the SUV anyway. Nothing—including a blizzard—was going to keep him from reaching Angela today.

"Angela."

The sound of her name made his heart sing. He stuffed an orange, an apple and a bag of cheese-flavored snacks in his jacket pockets, grabbed a bottle of water and a soda, locked up the house and ran to the garage.

God was so good! So good!

"Praise You, Jesus!" The shout echoed from the rafters. Hosea grinned. He couldn't stop grinning. And he couldn't stop praising the Lord—not that he wanted to.

He tossed his bag on the passenger seat, unloaded his pockets beside it, then climbed into the vehicle and inserted the key. At a twist of his wrist, the motor roared to life. "I'm coming, Angela! I'm on my way!"

Hosea laughed in sheer delight as he backed out of the drive and headed west. Six hours, maybe eight if the roads in the mountains were bad, and he would see her. He'd never let her get away again!

Angela placed her Bible on the coffee table and went to make a cup of tea to settle her nerves. Every time she thought of making that phone call tomorrow her stomach went into spasms. And that was getting to be her customary state since she'd done little but think about it since yesterday.

If only there was another way. Oh, Lord, if only there was another way.

The knock on the door startled her out of her thoughts. Angela jumped, then jerked around in the direction of the front door. Water hit the teapot she was filling and sprayed in every direction. She grabbed for the lever and shut off the tap.

"Bother! Now look at this mess!" She snatched the blue-checked dishtowel off its peg, wiped the droplets from her face, and blotted at the damp spots on the front of her sweater.

The knock sounded again.

"I'm coming!" Giving the counter a quick swipe with the towel, Angela hurried through the living room to the front door. "I'm sorry, Frank, I— Hosea!"

Her knees went weak. She took a wobbly step backward as he moved into the room. "How did you get here? I—I mean, how did you find me?"

"The Lord guided us. Cathy remembered about the retreat two years ago."

Hosea closed the door, then locked his gaze on hers. There was a look in his eyes she'd never seen before. Her heart began to thud.

"Why did you run away from me, Angela?"

She swallowed hard and took another step backward. His eyes looked like blue smoke! "I—I needed time alone…to pray."

"About us?"

So there it was. Angela's heart fluttered so wildly she thought it would fly away. She spun away from Hosea's steady, disconcerting gaze and walked to the middle of the living room. *Lord, I'm not ready for this! Why didn't You warn me? Why did You let him find me?*

Tears sprang into her eyes. She drew a deep breath, blinked the tears away and turned back to face Hosea. "Yes. I came here to pray about us. I may be wrong, but…well…I thought that night at Leigh and Phil's reception…you—" She swallowed past the lump in her throat and straightened to her full height. "I thought you were going to tell me you had feelings for me."

Blue flames flared deep in Hosea's eyes. Her breath caught.

"You're not wrong."

The soft, quietly spoken words brought such elation, such joy! But it was followed by pain so sharp and deep it made Angela gasp. She turned away.

"Did you receive an answer to your prayers?"

How could he be so calm when she was dying from

pain? "No. Yes! That is—I knew the answer all along." Her hands clenched into fists. "God didn't have to answer."

"I see."

Angela heard him remove his jacket and toss it on the sofa. How long would he stay? She bit down hard on her lower lip.

"And what is your answer?"

The pain hit her full force. She reached out and grabbed the back of a chair for support. "The answer is no. There can never be a personal relationship between us." *Please, Lord, let that be enough. Don't make me—*

"And why is that? Perhaps I'm wrong, but I thought you felt as I do." Hosea's voice softened, deepened. "*Am* I wrong, Angela? Is it that you don't care—" He stopped as a sob burst from her throat and she whirled around to face him.

"I was a prostitute, that's why!" She flung the words at him, then closed her eyes so she wouldn't have to see his face. *Oh, God, please, just make him go away. Just let this be over!*

"And what has that to do with our loving one another? With our getting married?"

"Married!" Angela's eyes flew open. "You're a *pastor,* Hosea! You can't marry a prostitute!" The words slashed like a knife through her heart. She gritted her teeth against the need to cry out—to yield to the pain.

"*Ex*-prostitute." Hosea quietly emphasized the word, then leaned down and picked up his jacket. "However, you're right—I am a pastor. And as such,

I cannot marry a woman lacking faith in God's grace and redemptive power.''

Angela couldn't have been more stunned if he had struck her. Mute with shock, she watched him zip his jacket.

He tugged the bottom into place and glanced at her. ''Is something wrong?''

A surge of anger broke the grip of the shock. ''Yes, there's something wrong! How dare you say such a thing to me? I am living proof of God's grace and redemptive power!'' Angela raised her chin a notch. ''Attack my character if you so choose, Hosea—but not my faith!''

''It was not an attack, Angela. Nonetheless, it's your faith that's lacking.'' He looked down and pulled his driving gloves from the right-hand pocket of his jacket. ''Peter had the same problem.''

''Peter?''

He gestured toward the Bible on the coffee table. ''Remember when Peter had the vision of a sheet full of all types of animals being lowered from heaven and the Lord told him to, 'Get up, Peter; kill and eat.''

Angela gave a tight little nod. ''Yes, I remember. But I don't see what—?''

''Peter refused. He said, 'By no means, Lord; for I have never eaten anything that is profane or unclean.' And the Lord answered him, 'What God has made clean, you must not call profane.''

Hosea's gaze bored into hers. ''The Lord was talking about people, Angela—not animals. They were only a symbol. When we ask Jesus to forgive our sin and come live in our hearts—when we are born

again—our past is dead and gone. We are a new crea-
ture in Him. God forgives and forgets. As His children
we are to do the same.'' His voice softened. ''You
need to do that, Angela. You need to stop calling unclean what God has cleansed. You need to accept His
forgiveness, forgive *yourself,* and forget the past—just
as He has done.''

Angela stared at him. She couldn't speak. Inside her
the truth of his words fought the grip of her past. Tears
flowed from her eyes and coursed down her cheeks.
She sank to her knees on the floor as the truth of re-
pentance washed over her.

''Oh, Lord, forgive, me. Forgive me for judging
myself unclean when in Your mercy You have forgiven and cleansed me of my past. Help me, Lord—
please give me the grace to forgive myself.''

The burden of guilt Angela had carried so long
lifted as the fetters with which she had bound herself
fell away. Peace flooded her heart. After a moment,
she wiped the tears from her face, gave Hosea a trem-
ulous smile, and rose to her feet. ''I—I don't know
what to say. Thank you, Hosea. Thank you for—''

He shook his head. ''Don't thank me, Angela, I'm
only the messenger. And this time—for the first
time—I had a selfish motive.''

That look was back in his eyes! Angela's stomach
jittered as he removed his jacket and stepped toward
her.

''Is the way clear for us, now? Are we going to be
all right?''

The love in his voice and eyes brought the world
crashing down around her. Angela's newfound peace

shattered. Her eyes filled. She loved him so much! She could never harm him. And what had just happened had not altered her past, only her future. Gathering all of her inner strength, she shook her head. ''No, Hosea. It could never work. If we married and the people in the church ever found out that I—''

''Not you, Angela…Gelina.''

Shock streaked through her. ''You *knew!*''

Hosea lifted his hand and gently wiped a tear from her cheek. ''Pastors develop an excellent memory for faces. It helps in our work. The subtle makeup and new hairstyle didn't fool me.''

''You knew from the start, and you still—''

Angela plopped down into the chair behind her, too astounded to grasp more than the fact that Hosea had fallen in love with her *knowing* her history. ''You knew….''

''That a prostitute named Gelina died in my presence, and a lovely young woman named Angela Warren was born again? Yes, I knew that.''

Hosea squatted on his heels in front of the chair and looked up at her. ''As for the congregation—if by some fluke any of them found out about the past and had a problem with it—I would tell them the same thing I have told you. Gelina is dead. The past is dead. God buried it. And it will stay buried forever. Only God has resurrection power, Angela—trust Him.'' His voice dropped to a husky whisper. ''Trust me.'' He rose to his feet and pulled her up into his arms.

''Wait!'' She stepped back, fastened her gaze on his. ''Before you… Before we—'' She drew a quick breath. "I need you to know that I never chose to live like that. I need you to know what happened."

"All right." Hosea took a firm grip on his emotions. His need to hold her, to have her safe in his arms, would have to wait. He released her hand.

Angela looked at him for a moment, then turned and walked to the window. "I never knew my father. He left when I was three years old. That's when Ben moved in. He and my mother were drug addicts." Her voice faltered. "My mother...sold herself...for money to keep their habits satisfied. There was little left for such things as food or clothing or rent, and we moved constantly because of the law." Her voice strengthened. "I had no other family that I knew of. And after a while my mother didn't register me for school because that would give authorities information about where they were, so I had no friends."

Hosea looked down at the floor, fighting back his need to pull her into his arms and comfort her.

"I couldn't go out during the day, because someone might see me and report that I wasn't in school, but I spent my late afternoons and evenings in the public library reading. When the library closed I would go back home, eat whatever I could find, and lock myself in my room and read. It helped to block out what my parents were doing in the other room."

Angela shuddered and wrapped her arms around herself. "And then one night—when I was twelve years old—I came home and went into my room. My key was gone."

Hosea stiffened. His hands clenched into fists. Angela went on, her hushed voice full of remembered terror.

"A strange man came into my room. I told him to get out, but he only laughed and reached for me. I ducked under his arm and ran for the door, but my mother and stepfather blocked my way. Ben grabbed me and held me. My mother said, 'Jack doesn't want me, Angela, he wants you. You want to help me don't you?' Then she patted my shoulder and said, 'Of course you do, you're such a good girl. So don't fight him, Angela. Just be good for me, and it will all be over soon.' Then Ben gave me to the man—and my mother closed and locked the door."

Something dark and ugly and scalding rose in Hosea. Rage blinded his vision. *Jesus, Lord, I need you!* The words rose in a desperate cry from his heart. The dark feeling left. His vision cleared. But anger remained.

"That was the beginning. I fought the men that came to my room. I fought them all. And I tried to run away, but my parents always found me—and then Ben would beat me. Sometimes the men that were waiting for me helped him."

Another shudder shook Angela's body. She was so pale it frightened him. Hosea stepped closer.

"And then, when I was fourteen, they sold me to Tony. He was their supplier. That's when I became Gelina. I tried to escape him, but he and his helpers were professionals. I was always caught and the beatings were worse. And then, one day, he told me if I tried to run away again he would kill me. So I hid away bonuses and tips he didn't know I had earned, took correspondence courses to get my GED, then registered for college using a P.O. Box. When I was accepted, I ran away again—under the threat of death. That's when I stumbled into the Crossroads church.''

Angela took a deep breath. The shuddering stopped. ''You know the rest. Except—'' Her gaze lifted to his face. ''You may not believe me, Hosea, but I've never been in a man's arms because I *wanted* to be there. I've loathed every touch, every minute, and…well… I'm nervous.'' She lifted her chin and looked him square in the eyes. ''I've never kissed a man. I'm not sure I'll know how.'' Her cheeks flamed with embarrassment. She looked away.

All the love for her Hosea had held in check so long rose up and drove the anger from him. What he had said was true. The past was dead and buried. The future was theirs. She was coming to him clean and pure. He would be no less for her. *Father God, I forgive them. I choose to forgive them all.* The words cleansed his heart and spirit.

He moved closer. ''I believe you.''

His voice! Angela's pulse quickened. She looked up and her whole body went weak at the look in Hosea's eyes. She swayed forward and his strong arms caught her, closed around her. He lowered his head and his mouth touched her ear. The heat of his lips made her shiver.

''I have the answer to your concern.''

The softly whispered words made her tingle. ''You do?''

''Yes…I do.''

The tingle shot all the way to her toes. "Wh-what is it?"

"Practice." Hosea brushed her lips with his. His arms tightened around her, drew her closer against him. His lips touched hers...hovered over them... claimed them. It was the first time she had ever been touched with love.

Of their own volition, Angela's arms slid up around Hosea's neck, her lips parted beneath his. With a soft sigh, she relaxed and gave herself up to the joy of being in his arms. It seemed she didn't have a problem after all.

Epilogue

Leigh fastened the gossamer veil in place and stepped back to make certain it was on straight. "Oh, Angela, you look so beautiful. You're absolutely radiant!" She laughed and wiped tears from her eyes. "I know that's a cliché, but in your case it's true. Oh, I'm so happy for you!"

Leigh threw her arms around Angela and hugged her, then again stepped back and wiped at her eyes. "Look at me! I'm an emotional mess. Its must be those having-a-baby hormones working overtime again." She patted her very pregnant belly and leaned against the table to take the weight off her feet. "Are you nervous?"

Angela took a deep breath and smiled. "Is there any tea in China?"

Leigh grinned. "Okay. It was a foolish question. Especially from someone—"

Both women turned at a polite *tap-tap*. The door opened slightly and Mary Stevens slid through the narrow space into the room. "I thought there should be a mother in here, and you don't qualify yet, Leigh." She laughed and turned toward Angela.

"Oh, my." Tears sprang into Mary's eyes. She lifted her hands to her cheeks, started to speak, then gave a small helpless wave of her hands in the air.

"Would you care to join me, Mrs. Stevens?" Leigh grinned and offered Hosea's mother the box of tissue on the table.

Mary Stevens laughed, plucked a tissue and dabbed at her eyes. "I promised myself I wouldn't do this. But you look so beautiful, Angela, my control just flew out the window." She smiled and moved closer. "I won't stay, dear. I know it's almost time and you have to finish preparing. I just wanted to tell you that Hosea is not the only one being blessed by his marriage to you today. Bill and I always wanted a second daughter, and now we'll have one lovelier inside and out, than we could ever have hoped for."

Angela swallowed hard. "Thank you, Mary."

"I'd be so pleased if you would make that Mom, Angela. When you're comfortable with it, of course."

Angela lost the battle. Tears pooled in her eyes and spilled over.

"Oh, Angela! Oh, I'm sorry, dear. I didn't mean to make you cry." Mary pulled her into her arms and held her close.

Leigh charged to the rescue. "Angela—quick! Think about Phil falling off the ladder in the nursery with the gallon of paint in his hands!"

It worked. Almost. There was an edge of nerves to Angela's laugh. But at least the tears stopped. She threw Leigh a look of gratitude. Leigh waggled her eyebrows. That did it. This time Angela's laughter was genuine.

Mary stepped back and smiled at Leigh. "I'm definitely going to have to hear that story later, but now—" she turned back to Angela "—I brought you something, dear. Please don't feel you must accept it. It's just something I thought of and—well, here."

Angela glanced down at Mary's outstretched hand. There was a penny on her palm.

"It's the penny I had in my shoe when I married Hosea's father. Hannah wanted her own, so I will understand perfectly if you don't want to— Oh, I've done it again!" Mary looked in dismay at the tears flowing down Angela's cheeks.

Angela didn't dare try to speak. She gave Mary a fierce hug, took the penny into her trembling hand, sat down on the bench in front of the makeup table and removed her shoe. Shaking out the penny that was in it, she placed Mary's penny inside.

"Hello in there!" The soft call came as the door opened the merest slit. "Mary, it's time. The usher is waiting to seat you."

"All right, Bill—I'm coming." Mary leaned down and kissed Angela on the cheek, then grabbed a handful of tissues and walked to the door. "Know our love is walking down the aisle with you, dear." The door closed on her whispered words.

"Wow! What a wonderful woman. No wonder Hosea is such a great guy." Leigh blotted her eyes and grinned at Angela, who looked ready to burst into tears again. "Let's lighten things up a bit, shall we? The atmosphere is pretty thick in here, and my hormones won't take it. Did I ever tell you about Phil's head-to-head confrontation with the concierge at our hotel in Paris?''

Leigh walked over and sat down on the bench beside Angela to examine her face in the mirror for tear damage. ''Yikes! What a mess!'' She reached for a tissue and wiped the smudges of black mascara off her cheeks, while Angela turned around on the bench. Their gazes met in the mirror. Leigh smiled and handed her a tissue.

''It all started because Phil insisted he knew how to speak French....''

The music stopped. Leigh, Cathy and Diane had reached the altar. Angela took a firmer grip on the bouquet in her hands as the musical chords that were their signal sounded.

''Ready, princess?''

Angela took a deep breath as John Scott smiled at her. She slid her hand through his offered arm and nodded. The ushers pulled open the double doors.

Step—pause—step. Step—pause—step. Angela thought her trembling legs would collapse as they started down the aisle. She lifted her gaze to where Frank and Greta stood smiling at her, glanced at Sophie who was playing the piano, and then looked down the aisle to where Hosea stood waiting for her. Her heart filled with joy, and suddenly the walk was much too slow. She wanted to run to him.

Hosea nodded to Sophie and the music softened. Angela's heart pounded as he fastened his gaze on hers and held out his hand. His voice and eyes bathed her with love as he began speaking God's beautiful words from the book of Hosea.

"'I will betroth you to me forever; I will betroth you in righteousness and justice, in love and compassion. I will betroth you in faithfulness....'

His strong, warm hand closed over hers, and in that instant, an unshakeable certainty flooded her soul. This was why God called him here—to bless us both with love.

Angela's heart swelled. At last, she had her answer. A beautiful calm filled her. She blinked her tears away, handed her bouquet to Leigh, and turned back to her beloved. Their gazes met. She smiled. Hosea's hand tightened on hers, and together they walked up the steps to the altar.

Dear Reader,

Writing *Hosea's Bride* was quite an experience for me. Angela's struggle to build a meaningful life for herself despite the burden of guilt and pain she carried hidden inside was at once inspiring and heartrending. It made me wonder how many of us share Angela's plight? How many of us walk through life burdened by the guilt of past sin the Lord has *long ago* forgiven and cast into His *"forgetting sea"*? It also made me realize how important it is to follow the Lord's example and forgive others and, sometimes, our own selves most of all.

And then there was Hosea. Ah, Hosea! I confess I adore him. I love his quiet strength, his caring heart and that lovely sense of humor that peeks out every so often. But, most of all, I love him because he's so human! Hosea's struggle to understand God's will and then yield to it in spite of the desires of his own heart is one I believe we can all identify with. Jesus said, "Watch and pray that ye enter not into temptation: the spirit indeed is willing, but the flesh is weak." How well He knows us! And how awesome is His love for us.

And last, as a reader I understand that selecting and buying a book is a very personal thing. Thank you for choosing *Hosea's Bride*. I hope it was an enjoyable and uplifting reading experience for you. I would enjoy hearing from you. I can be reached at dorothyjclark@hotmail.com.

Until next time,

Dorothy Clark

HEART AND SOUL

BY

JILLIAN HART

Taking in an injured stranger wasn't something
Michelle McKaslin would normally do, but she'd
sensed something special about Gabe Brody. But
would her heaven-sent feelings remain when she
learned who he really was—the undercover agent
investigating her family?

Don't miss

HEART AND SOUL
On sale May 2004.

Available at your favorite retail outlet.

Visit us at www.steeplehill.com   LIHAS

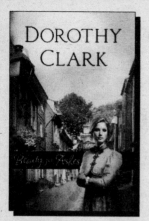

DOROTHY CLARK

Steeple Hill Books brings you a sweeping historical saga of faith, forgiveness and loving by

DOROTHY CLARK

Available June 2004.

Visit us at www.steeplehill.com

SDC515CAN

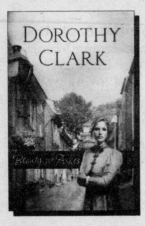

Steeple Hill Books brings you a sweeping historical saga of faith, forgiveness and loving by

DOROTHY CLARK

Available June 2004.

Save $1.00 off the purchase price of *Beauty for Ashes*.

Redeemable at participating retailers in the U.S. only. May not be combined with other coupons or offers.

RETAILER: Steeple Hill Books will pay the face value of this coupon plus 8 cents if submitted by the customer for this specified product only. Any other use constitutes fraud. Coupon is non-assignable, void if taxed, prohibited or restricted by law. Consumer must pay for any government taxes. Valid in the U.S. only. Mail to: Harlequin Enterprises Ltd., Steeple Hill Books, P.O. Box 880478, El Paso, TX 88588-0478, U.S.A. Non-NCH retailers—for reimbursement submit coupons and proof of sales directly to: Steeple Hill Books, Retail Marketing Dept., 225 Duncan Mill Rd., Don Mills (Toronto), Ontario M3B 3K9, Canada. Cash value 1/100 cents. Limit one coupon per customer.

Coupon is valid until December 31, 2004.

Manufacturer's coupon

Steeple Hill®

5 65373 00076 2 (8100) 0 11121

® is a registered trademark of Harlequin Enterprises Ltd. or its affiliates. © 2003 Harlequin Enterprises Ltd.

Visit us at www.steeplehill.com

SDC515US